THE SECRET ARCHIVES TRILOGY
BOOK ONE

THE
DOCILES

VALERIE PURI

First Edition. Printed in the United States of America.
ISBN-13: 978-1732482500 | ISBN-10: 1732482500

Editing Services Provided by
Brass Rag Press and Juli's Elite Editing

Cover Created by Covers by Christian

Interior Formatting by Rene Folsom with Phycel Designs

SYNOPSIS

Walls are meant to keep the monsters out...

Deep in the forest there is a wall where no wall should be. Behind it live the people of the Commune, the last remnant of human kind.

Jennie Caraway has lived behind the wall her entire life, certain that it protects her and her brother from the lemerons, ravenous undead monsters whose only desire is to kill – and feed.

Jennie's peaceful existence is shattered when she uncovers a secret organization whose purpose threatens to destroy not only Jennie, but her entire world. The Order has a deadly mission, and they will stop at nothing to see it completed.

Jennie and those closest to her must expose the evil truth before they are killed – or worse.

For my husband

TABLE OF CONTENTS

PROLOGUE

The icy rain felt like blades slicing into the ranger's face as it came down diagonally in heavy sheets. His green tunic was drenched and he was chilled to the bone. The treacherous storm cast everything into penetrating darkness. Unease filled the ranger as he maneuvered his way through the thick, mangled forest. The howling wind was just audible over the deafening barrage of rain beating against his soaked hood.

Lightning ripped across the sky, giving a momentary burst of light accompanied by thunderous booming. The heart of the storm was growing closer and more violent. During the brief illumination, the ranger tried to orient himself and gain an understanding of his location. He could only make out the small portion of forest which was close enough to avoid being distorted by the heavy rainfall.

A flash slashed through the clouds. He saw the surrounding trees again and made his way forward. By the light he could see movement in the bushes ahead. At first, he thought it little more than the wind blowing in the underbrush. The next flash of lightning changed his mind.

Emerging from the bushes was a skeletal figure. It was coming toward him with a slow, determined pace like an animal stalking its prey. An animal would run from the ranger. However, this was no animal. The ranger froze in his tracks. This was the creature he feared most.

It was closing the distance between them. The ranger had to get away before it was too late.

CHAPTER 1

A chill was in the air that autumn morning as Jennie Caraway started out of her house to tend to her work. The days were growing shorter, and the sun had yet to rise over the top of the wall encircling the Commune. Jennie didn't mind the dimness that surrounded her as it was always before dawn when she started her day. It was five o'clock in the morning, judging by the position of the constellations in the sky. She could always mark the time by the stars – a talent her father said she inherited from her mother.

Jennie ambled along the cobblestone path shrouded in deep, purple shadows. The muffled tapping of her leather boots was all that could be heard in the silence preceding dawn. She walked by a gap between neighboring homes, and a gust of wind made her shiver. Jennie pulled the ends of her sweater sleeves over her hands and folded her arms tightly against her body. Her favorite maroon sweater did little to stop the wind, and she silently cursed herself for not wearing her coat.

As she walked the familiar route by memory, Jennie passed small cottage homes identical to the one she shared with her father and younger brother. Her father, Jack Caraway, had previously been one of the hunters who often braved the forest and the darkness within. No one left the Commune anymore – not even the hunters – so her father now worked as a blacksmith, making tools for the farmers. Her brother, Travis, was only twelve and still too young to select a profession. Until he came of age, Travis helped in the Commune kitchen, preserving food for winter.

The cottages gave way to more substantial stone, and brick buildings as Jennie neared the town's center. She crossed the square and made her way past the towering building known as the Sanctuary. The impressive structure situated at the center of town had stately appeal. Tall white, columns stood like sentries at the front entrance. A tower emerged majestically from the center of the lower portion of the structure, making it the tallest building in the Commune.

Like all the townspeople of the Commune, she frequented the lower levels of the Sanctuary where weekly Commune Councils took place. Despite entering the building numerous times, Jennie had never entered the Sanctuary's tower where the two Elders lived. Glancing up, she wondered how far someone could see from the top of the soaring structure.

A faint light glowing from one of the high tower windows caught her eye. The window faced westward, the only opening on that side of the tower. She thought the light was strange at this early hour. Dismissing it as nothing more than a gas lamp someone forgot to extinguish, Jennie continued toward the stables located on the opposite side of town.

The horses had to be tended to before the others awoke to begin their daily work. During the peak farming months, Jennie had to have the horses ready for when the farmers came for them at first light. As it was late fall, the horses wouldn't be needed until the final harvest in two weeks' time. It was easier on both her and the horses if she kept her usual schedule.

She took pleasure in this time of year. She was able to enjoy her uninterrupted time with the animals she loved. When the horses were working the fields, her work in the stables was lonely. The presence of the gentle beasts of burden comforted her. They reminded her of her mother. So when the horses were with the farmers, she felt the emptiness of the stables reflected the emptiness within.

Her mother had been the previous Stable Head and, when Jennie was younger, she would often come along to help. She had worked with the horses for as long as she could remember and it was the highlight of her morning.

As she walked through the square, the water trickling softly in the fountain brought her memories forward. She recalled how her mother always said the horses seemed to be soothed by Jennie, how it was her special talent. She never thought her abilities were different from anyone else's. The Elders seemed to recognize her gift, however, for they named her Stable Head at the age of thirteen after her mother had… Jennie shuddered and pushed the thought from her mind.

She focused on the wind, likening it to the feel of cold feathers brushing against her face. She cocked her head, listening to the sound the trees made as the branches rustled in the wind. After putting distance between herself and the town square – and memories of her mother – she walked between two rows of apple trees. Reaching up, she grasped an apple. A gentle shower of morning dew shook free from the branch, which snapped back into place after freeing the apple. Jennie dried her dew-dampened hand and dropped the apple into the tan bag hanging from her shoulder.

The familiar scent of hay, grain, and horses welcomed Jennie as she entered the stables. The building was a wooden structure with numerous stalls lining each side of a central aisle. The horses liked to poke their heads out of their stalls to greet Jennie as she walked by. Above was the hayloft accessible only by a wooden ladder in the middle of the building.

She walked up to the first stall on her left. "Good morning, Misty," she said to the chestnut mare who came to the opening above the wooden gate.

She reached into her bag and pulled out the glossy red apple. With a flat hand, she held it out to the mare. The whiskers on Misty's chin tickled her palm as the horse gratefully took the sweet treat with her lips, crunching it between her teeth.

"You're coming along nicely," Jennie said, more to the mare's pregnant stomach than to the horse herself. Misty threw her head up and down in a playful manner as if agreeing with her. The exchange warmed Jennie's heart. She felt rejuvenated from the cold and was ready to begin her work.

CHAPTER 2

Travis Caraway woke with a start. His bed sheets were saturated in sweat. He was only eight when he lost his mother, but his recurring nightmares made him relive the terror. Since that day four years ago, his family had never been whole. He shuddered. He was afraid of being taken by them too.

He sat up in bed, rubbing his eyes in an attempt to erase the nightmare from his mind. Glancing across the room, he saw Jennie's bed - empty and neatly made.

Travis put on charcoal grey pants and pulled a blue sweater on over his head. He left the room he shared with his sister and entered the washroom. A ragged stranger with bloodshot eyes peered back at him from the mirror. Splashing cold water on his face, he let the remnants of his dream drip away. He dried his face and combed out his short, brown hair. Scrutinizing his reflection, Travis felt he looked a little better now. He could almost fool himself into believing he felt better as well.

He walked into the kitchen and found his breakfast waiting on the table. Jennie always prepared porridge for him and their father before she left. Travis and his father usually ate breakfast together, but only one bowl remained on the wooden table. Realizing he must have overslept, Travis frantically spooned the cold mush into his mouth and placed the dirty bowl in the kitchen sink. He knew he would be scolded for not washing his dish, but he would face that later.

He threw his bag over his shoulder, and dashed out of the house. His school was in the town center, and it would only take five minutes to get there if he ran. He hated running but didn't have time for the extra ten minutes it would take to walk the distance. He could not afford to be late to school again.

Being late was frowned upon in the Commune. The two Elders often taught how the Commune was the last refuge of mankind and how its success was indeed built on punctuality.

"If the blacksmiths are not punctual, we do not have tools for the workers. If the farmers are not punctual, we do not yield a good crop. If the students are not punctual, we will not have our future." This was Victor Glassman's favorite speech during the weekly Commune Council. He always said the last part while staring directly at where the children were designated to sit, almost daring any one of them to go against his words.

Despite the chill in the air, sweat formed on Travis' brow. With a clumsy effort, he checked his watch and was relieved to see only four minutes had passed. He'd run faster than he thought.

The school was a square building with three floors, constructed of red bricks and large white corner stones. The copper dome, now green with age, housed the only bell in the Commune. It's metallic ringing signaled the beginning and end of school sessions and the weekly Commune Council. Fortunately for Travis, the bell hadn't rung yet. He wasn't late.

Travis thrust the weight of his slight body into the school's wooden front door, pushing it open. Students were still mingling in the corridors, and Travis was relieved he had made it in time. Trying to control the heaving of his lungs, he stepped inside and let the door close with a thud behind him.

CHAPTER 3

Jennie watched Travis enter the school's assembly hall seconds before the bell rang, signaling the start of the morning session. The robust door slammed shut with an echo that reverberated against the bare walls and hard tables in the chamber. She caught her brother's eye and, with a small wave, invited him to sit next to her at the long table she shared with four other students. Travis looked distraught as he crossed the large room with his head down. He had almost been late, and from his appearance it was apparent he'd run to school. Jennie knew he overslept because of the nightmare. It worried her that they were growing more frequent.

"Same dream?" Jennie asked Travis quietly, as he collapsed into the vacant metal chair next to her.

"Yes," he replied breathlessly.

"That's three times this week. Why do you think the dreams are happening so often?"

"Working in the kitchen doesn't help. Those monsters' eyes are the same. I don't care if the ones here are harmless," he murmured weakly with downcast eyes.

Jennie put her hand on his arm to console him. "I know," she said almost a whisper. "I know."

"How is Misty doing?" Travis asked, clearly trying to change the subject.

"She's going to have her foal any day now. Want to come watch?"

With Misty about to give birth to her foal, Jennie spent more time at the stables and less at home. Perhaps having Travis spend time at the stables might help him. It helped her.

He managed a smile. "Sure, that would be great."

The school principal began speaking at the small podium across the room. Jennie and Travis fell silent so they wouldn't receive looks from the teachers standing at the edges of the room. The announcement that school would not be in session next week to commemorate the founding of the Commune received cheers from all the students. Jennie was glad she would have more time to spend with Misty and the other horses. The bell rang dismissing the students, and they made their way to their classes on the second floor.

Jennie walked Travis to his classroom, stopping outside the room with "Level 7" inscribed on the door. He kept his eyes on his shoes.

"Try not to think about it," Jennie said, sensing that her brother was still troubled. "You won't have to work in the kitchen much longer if you don't want to. You'll be thirteen in a couple days, and then you can choose whatever work you want." She smiled reassuringly at Travis then added, "You can even choose to help me in the stables."

Travis nodded and walked through the door. Jennie continued down the hall and entered the door labeled "Level 11." At seventeen, Jennie was in her final year of school. Once finished, she would be able to spend her entire day working and would even be eligible to become an Advisor to the Elders. Not everyone chose to be an Advisor or even the head of their profession. Pride swelled inside her.

Inside the classroom, Jennie slid into her seat at the front of the room. The metal chair was cold and gave her goose bumps when she sat down. She was glad the attached desk was made of wood. It gave her a slightly warmer place to rest her arms. She was still regretting her decision not to wear her coat.

The seat next to her was conspicuously empty and she wondered where Belle was. Jennie and Belle Joiner had been best friends since they were in level one. Jennie hadn't seen Belle in the morning session either. It was not like her to be late and especially not to miss an entire session.

The teacher, Mrs. Townsend, strode into the room purposefully. Without speaking, she walked straight to the chalkboard to write today's topic of discussion. Mrs. Townsend was tall and had a curvy figure which was accentuated by her blue dress. Jennie admired the stiff woven fabric of the knee-length dress she was wearing. It looked crisp and new, and most of all, warm.

Mrs. Townsend's brown hair fell elegantly to her shoulders and bounced slightly as her arm shot up and down while she wrote. Once finished, she folded her arms and stepped to the side to reveal the phrase written on the board: "Life Before the Commune." The word "Before" was underlined. The class let out a collective gasp. This was a forbidden topic, and Mrs. Townsend knew it.

"Class, how many of you know what life was like *before* the Commune?"

No hands went up.

"How many of you have seen texts from before our three-hundred-acre paradise was created? Who can tell me how we were founded?"

A small hand went up timidly.

"Yes, Miss. Caraway?" Mrs. Townsend pointed to Jennie with the chalk.

Jennie reluctantly regurgitated what Elder Victor had always taught at the Commune Council. "It is said," she began, "that the last survivors of humankind came together in this forest searching for food, shelter, and safety. They found, in the heart of the forest, a clearing with a small cluster of buildings. They took shelter in the structures and found peace in the clearing. Using stones from a nearby quarry, they erected a wall surrounding the area and established the Commune as the last sanctuary of humankind. They tilled the land, bred livestock, and harnessed the power of the sun to generate electricity, thus creating a self-sustaining way of life."

Jennie saw Mrs. Townsend was nodding along. When her teacher did not speak, Jennie took that as permission to continue.

"They proclaimed that the Commune would be led by two Elders – one male and one female – who would appoint their own successors. A weekly council would be held with all those who dwell within the Commune present. All townspeople, Profession Heads, and Advisors would have an equal voice, helping to guide the Elders in making decisions which preserve the longevity of the Commune. And so, for two-hundred years, this has been our way of life."

Jennie always thought the story of the Commune's origin had too many holes in it. How many people were in the original group? Where did they come from? How could they manage to build such a tall wall encircling such a large area? How did the founders choose the first Elders when there were no predecessors? How did the dociles get in? And most importantly, how could the founders have been so sure they were the last humans left?

Jennie wanted to ask Mrs. Townsend these things, but she heard her father's voice in her head. "Your curiosity will get you into serious trouble one day, Jennie. There are some things you should not go digging into." This always unsettled her and for years her questions remained unasked.

"Very good," Mrs. Townsend said, snapping Jennie back into the present. "This is the founding we have all been taught. But this is only a *part* of the story."

The students all looked at each other with wide, questioning gazes. No one had ever made such a statement before. Jennie leaned forward in her chair with a surge of excitement.

"You have never been taught about where we came from. What I am about to show you is from the Secret Archives of our society."

The class was murmuring when Mrs. Townsend mentioned "Secret Archives," No one had heard of such a thing. Their teacher held up her hand for silence, "I have for you the full story."

Mrs. Townsend dimmed the lights and turned on the projector. An image appeared on the screen at the front of the class. It was a picture of a group of people standing just outside of the school building. There were about seventy-five of them, three rows of roughly twenty-five people each. Some were holding shovels, some holding large knives, and some with bows; their quivers of arrows slung over their backs.

Jennie had never seen any of these people before nor such an arsenal of weapons. Their clothing consisted of tattered fabrics in muted colors, giving one the impression they had all worn these same clothes for numerous years. There was nothing remarkable about any of their faces, except that one seemed familiar to her.

Mrs. Townsend continued to speak. "These are our founders. They took this photo roughly two hundred years ago. Every twenty-five years, a photo is taken of the entire population of the Commune. We are told they are used to catalog our population growth for future generations, so they can learn how we continued to increase our resource yield, meeting the needs of our growing society. However, few have ever been shown these photos, because the images reveal too much. Hence, why they were in the Secret Archives."

Mrs. Townsend started clicking her hand-held device to progress through the photos, each taken twenty-five years apart. Some of the faces repeated, looking older with the passage of time. As she clicked through the images, Mrs. Townsend continued the tale.

"You will notice that the faces age and new faces are added as families grow. But has anyone spotted the one anomaly?"

Mrs. Townsend's eyes scanned the class as if entreating someone to answer. Murmurs of confusion filled the room behind Jennie. She slumped in her chair, trying to become invisible. She had spotted it - spotted her – but she was too shaken to speak.

"There is one face which never changes, never grows old, and is in every photo. She is here in this corner." Mrs. Townsend pointed to the woman Jennie recognized. "She is one of our Elders, Marlene Saunders."

CHAPTER 4

Jennie walked to the school cafeteria in a daze. Her mind felt numb. *Could it be true?* she thought. It was common knowledge that the monsters didn't age. *Elder Marlene wasn't a monster, was she?* Jennie shook her head, dismissing the idea. *She couldn't be one of them*, she thought, trying to convince herself.

After picking up her food tray from the counter, she made her way to her usual lunch table. She spotted the back of Belle's head with her unmistakable frizzy, tight curls. Her best friend never changed; Belle was still the same bubbly, brilliant girl Jennie had met nearly eleven years ago.

"Hey Belle." she said.

"Hey," Belle said brightly. "Wait, what's gotten into you? You look…" She paused and squinted at Jennie. "Disturbed."

"I've never been good at masking my feelings, have I? Where were you this morning? You missed some really heavy stuff."

"I had to work late at the solar farm. We had to replace some dead solar cells. Routine stuff really, but when we got in there to check it out, all the cables were chewed through. Rats probably." Belle scrunched her nose while stabbing at her beans with a fork. "We had to rip out the whole sector of panels and replace all the cables. It was not fun. Trust me, I would have rather been in class."

Belle worked at the solar farm which generated the electricity used to provide key buildings in the Commune with power. The only buildings that had electric lights and conduits were the school, medical and science facilities, and the lower levels in the Sanctuary. There weren't enough solar panels to power all the buildings, houses included, with electricity.

"So, what did I miss?" Belle asked.

Jennie summarized the morning lesson for Belle. She even shared her half-formed thoughts about Marlene somehow being like the monsters. Belle listened intently with her mouth agape.

"But," Belle began, "it can't be. Maybe the woman in the pictures isn't the same woman at all. Maybe they're all Marlene's ancestors. I mean, she can't be a monster, she doesn't even look like one."

"You're right. She doesn't have the grey, blotchy skin, the green-tinged lips, or the yellow eyes." Jennie shuddered. "But it's just too strange. Come on, finish your food. You need to see it for yourself."

The girls hurriedly ate their food and dashed out of the cafeteria. They still had about fifteen minutes left before the next session started.

As they walked quickly down the hall towards their classroom, Belle said, "If this is true, I can see how it's a bit shocking to find out that one of your Elders has eternal life, or however you want to put it. But technically, it's not teaching the forbidden subject. Mrs. Townsend only taught what happened at the time of the Commune's founding and what came after. Although, it *is* a little out of synch with how history is usually taught."

Jennie chuckled as she thought of how she parroted the Commune's history to the class. It was vague and drilled into them in a repetitively.

"Yeah. I bet if Elder Victor found out about today's lesson he wouldn't be happy. Anyway, before dismissing us for lunch, Mrs. Townsend said this was to 'prime our minds.' During the afternoon session she's going to teach us about what happened before the founding."

They reached the door to their classroom and stepped inside. Mrs. Townsend was sitting at her desk reading a worn book, "Ah. Jennie, Belle, come in, please. We missed you during class this morning, Belle," she said, closing the book rather quickly.

"Sorry about that. There were some unexpected issues down at the solar farm. I have a note from my superior," Belle handed Mrs. Townsend a paper from her pocket.

"Mrs. Townsend, we were hoping you would let Belle see the photos you showed the class this morning."

"I have no idea what you are talking about." Mrs. Townsend said coolly. Her eyes darted toward the door and back to them.

Mrs. Townsend hastily opened her desk drawer, extracted the photos, and placed them in between the pages of the book she'd been reading. She then thrust the book, pictures and all, into Jennie's hands.

"Thank you, Belle, for the note. I will be sure to mark your absence this morning as excused," Mrs. Townsend motioned to Jennie's bag.

Jennie quickly stuffed the tattered book into her bag. She and Belle stared at each other with raised eyebrows, wondering what was happening.

The classroom door swung open. In stepped a man with a shaved head. The dark clothing he wore made his pale skin seem nearly translucent. His broad shoulders were slightly hunched forward as if weighed down by his muscular arms. His gaze was cold, staring at them with dark, beady eyes.

Jennie recognized him right away. He was Jacob Sash, a key Advisor to Elder Victor. His presence made her stomach turn over. He narrowed his gaze at Jennie and Belle. His lips pressed into a thin line. The way he glared at them made her wish she were still in the cafeteria, far away from him.

"Thank you for stopping by girls. You can have a two-day extension on your assignment. I suggest you go and start working on it now," Mrs. Townsend said, dismissing them casually.

When Jennie turned to leave, she noticed the word "before" on the chalkboard had been erased and replaced with "inside". The topic "Life Inside the Commune" was an accepted one and taught often. Jennie wondered what had happened to make Mrs. Townsend change it.

As Jennie and Belle closed the door behind them, they heard Sash say to Mrs. Townsend, "You have done a very bad thing Eleanor. You've upset some very important people. They want to see you now."

CHAPTER 5

With head held high, Eleanor Townsend walked alongside Sash who had come to take her away. He had a firm grip on her right arm, and she knew it would leave a mark. His dark, recessed eyes were fixed ahead and his thin lips were set in a stern frown. She recalled that Sash was not a very friendly man; his personality was in stark contrast to the rest of the residents of the Commune.

Eleanor had known that sooner or later they would send someone for her, but she had not expected it to be this soon. Her task was to reveal the hidden knowledge to her students, then to the rest of the Commune. But her time had been cut short. *You can't just break into the Secret Archives and not expect anyone to find ou*t, she thought.

* * *

Early that morning, before anyone else was awake, Eleanor slipped through a side door of the Sanctuary. She made her way to the tower entrance on the third floor. The door leading to the tower was usually closed, but it stood open. She bit her lower lip, wondering if it was safe to proceed. Swallowing her apprehension, she took her lantern from the bag hanging at her side and lit the wick with a match.

In the dancing light of the flame, she ascended the cold, stone spiral staircase. She ran her hand along the wall as she continued to climb, counting each step as she did so. She stopped at the step where her husband said the door would be, the door to the Secret Archives. Sorrow gripped at her heart as she thought of her husband, James. He hadn't made it this far.

They took him after he discovered what they were doing. When he refused to participate, they made him disappear. He was a scientist working on a serum to restore the dociles back to their human state. James was reviewing his earlier research when he discovered someone changed his records. His superiors had taken his life's work and tainted it. They wanted to create more dociles.

Eleanor stood in the darkness in front of the door. She clenched her fist when she thought about the horrors her husband uncovered. She had planned this moment carefully – it was one month to the day after her husband's disappearance. She would find proof of the corruption within the Commune and share it with the brightest minds of the new generation: her students.

The door to the Secret Archives was constructed to appear as a continuation of the curved wall in the staircase, but the mark scratched into the stone was unmistakable. In the dim light of her lantern, she ran her fingers over the etched symbol. She traced the outline of a rearing horse inside of a circle. *This is it,* she thought.

Eleanor placed her palms on the symbol and pushed with all of her strength. Despite the stone door's weight, it opened with ease. A sudden rush of cold air enveloped her and threatened to extinguish the flame of her lantern. She entered the Secret Archives where the scent of aged, musty books welcomed her.

* * *

Eleanor stumbled as Sash aggressively pulled her forward. His unfaltering grip on her arm caused her fingers to tingle from lack of blood circulation. They walked across the cobblestone square, which marked the center of the Commune, and up to the main entrance of the Sanctuary.

Eleanor scanned the open area but saw no one. People in the Commune always ate together in the dining hall at this time of day, so she was not surprised to find the lively square completely vacant. She was alone.

Sash led Eleanor into the Sanctuary and up the stairs. He pulled her past the door leading to the tower where she had just been earlier that morning. She wondered if they had even bothered to take her husband here before they made him disappear. It would have been ironic for James to be brought so close to where the Secret Archives were stored only for him to be disposed of. Eleanor's upper lip twitched with rage as she thought of the injustice committed against her husband. She would do anything to get him back and see those responsible brought to justice.

Sash thrust Eleanor into one of the small meeting rooms. She stumbled forward from the force. A tall man with broad shoulders and grey hair stood at the opposite end of the room facing the window with his hands held behind his back. His silhouette was dark against the bright day outside. As he turned to face her, she did not recognize him right away. It wasn't until he spoke that she realized she was looking at Victor Glassman. *Victor the Elder.*

"Eleanor Townsend, do you know why you are here?" he asked, his deep voice crisp and commanding.

"No," she lied.

A chilling smile spread across his face. "How amusing."

He gestured for Eleanor to sit at the table between them. Sash shoved her toward the chair, and she sat down reluctantly. She was still too stunned by Victor presence to be able to fully comprehend what it could mean. *How far up did this plot go?* she wondered.

Victor continued. "A trusted informant of mine provided me with details of your activities this morning. My informant saw a light in the west window of the tower. There is only one window on that side of the tower, and it belongs to the Secret Archives," he paused and tapped his finger against his lips, feigning thinking, "but I think you already knew that."

"I assure you, I have no idea about any Secret Archives," she said, shaking her head.

She thought about the pictures and the book she had stolen from the Secret Archives earlier that morning. *Jennie will figure out what to do with them.* Eleanor thought, *she is smart, and we have the same motive, even if she doesn't realize it yet.*

"My informant also tells me once the light faded from the window, you walked out of the Sanctuary less than five minutes later." His voice had an edge of impatience.

"I was under the impression there were going to be others here," Eleanor said coolly. "Where are they?"

"They do not need to be here. I speak for my counterparts, and do not interrupt me." Victor replied. "Now tell me, why were you in the Secret Archives this morning? What did you take? Who did you tell?"

"Again, I don't..."

Victor slammed both of his hands on the table, yelling, "Do not lie to me."

Sash stood in the corner of the room behind Victor, his arms crossed in front of his chest and wearing a smirk on his face. Eleanor could tell from his body language that he was enjoying this.

"Accessing the Secret Archives is forbidden. Stealing is forbidden. Spreading your lies is forbidden." Victor's voice was now a harsh shouting.

"My lies?" Eleanor questioned hotly. "What about *your* lies."

"We have never lied to our people. We have only done what is best to preserve our way of life."

"The omission of the truth is just another way to lie." Eleanor lost all control. There was no possible way of getting out of this situation. Regardless, she still wanted answers. "Tell me," she demanded, "what about preserving the lives of those who oppose you? Why don't you tell the Commune about where people really go when they disappear? What about my husband's disappearance?"

Victor's face flushed red with anger. He stepped back from the table and nodded over his shoulder at Sash. Sash approached her and took a black, cloth sack from his back pocket. In one swift motion, he threw it over Eleanor's head, tightening the strings around her neck.

She gasped, and fabric was pulled into her mouth by the sharp intake of air. She felt something sharp poke her in the arm. Her hearing became muffled, her head began to spin, and then everything went cold.

Eleanor Townsend was no more.

CHAPTER 6

The ranger lay on a bed of hay trying to ignore the pain in his body. It was incredibly warm inside the building, and he wasn't sure if it was from the wooden walls blocking the wind or his fever. Probably his fever, he decided miserably. Staring up at the wooden beams supporting the roof, he thought about how he had almost lost his life. It had been two days since that terrifying night.

* * *

The ranger had feared he might risk encountering a lemeron that night; anyone who came too close to one rarely lived to tell the tale. The torrential rains and the intense darkness had made it nearly impossible for him to see. As he ventured through the blackness, finding his way with his outstretched hands, he couldn't shake the feeling something bad was about to happen.

That's when the lightning began, giving him intermittent visibility. He saw the skeletal figure stagger forward becoming visible through the heavy rain. The blotchy-grey flesh of the lemeron sagged from its bones and hung like ill-fitting clothing. It released a guttural moan causing the ranger to go rigid.

When he saw the lemeron approaching him, the ranger turned and hurried in a new direction, one perpendicular to his previous course. After putting some distance between himself and the monster, the ranger took care to disguise himself in the underbrush growing beneath a tall tree. He gazed in the direction he had just come from to see if the lemeron followed him. The loud pounding of his heart in his ears made him aware of its rapid pace. He tried to slow his heart rate if only to hear better, but it was to no avail.

He was startled by a crack behind him, the sound of a stick breaking underfoot. His fear turned to terror as he felt a boney hand seize his left arm. As the ranger spun around, the firm grip tightened, and sharp fingernails pierced his skin. The blood drained from his face at the sight. He was staring into the grey, sagging face of a lemeron.

He struggled and tried to pull away from the monster, but the action only made it clench tighter, its fingernails digging deeper and deeper into his arm. The cloudy, yellow eyes of the lemeron were wide and hungry. Its green lips parted, exposing blackened teeth. It lunged at him with its fully bared teeth.

The ranger was certain he would die in that moment. He frantically grabbed for the dagger hanging from his belt, his trembling fingers wrapped around the cold handle. He drew the blade from its sheath and instinctively swung it upward. His attack cut diagonally through the lemeron's chest, sending it stumbling backward, but it was not enough for the monster to release him. Brown, congealed blood oozed from the rotting flesh. The ranger raised his dagger high above his head, and with all his strength, brought the blade down. His aim was good, and the small blade sliced through the monster's wrist, severing the hand, thus releasing the ranger from its grasp. A crackling groan escaped from its throat, not from pain – lemerons feel no pain – but from anger.

The ranger ran mindlessly through the darkness, stumbling over the tangle of slippery roots covering the forest floor. He had to put as much distance between himself and the lemeron as possible. He smashed into a tree, not noticing it was in his path. Searing pain exploded through his left shoulder, and a rush of warm liquid ran down his arm. *It must be my blood*, he thought. His arm felt like it was on fire, but he could not stop to tend to it. He could hear the beast crashing through the underbrush behind him.

His head pounded, his heart raced, adrenalin surged through his veins, and his muscles begged him to stop running. Suddenly he slammed into something massive. The force of the impact knocked him on his back and the air rushed from his lungs. Dazed, he lay on the soaked ground while the freezing raindrops battered his face. He remained horizontal and motionless until he was able to recover his breath and regain control of his limbs.

The ranger stood up and reached his hand out in front of him to feel what had stopped him. The oppressive night was growing ever darker as the storm raged; he could barely see his hand in front of his face. He touched something smooth and hard – it felt like stone. Lightning ripped across the sky in a spider web of brilliant streaks. In the prolonged flash, the ranger saw a stone wall extending as far as he could see in either direction.

He was trapped. His only options were to go backward or to go forward. Behind him was the lemeron, and in front of him was a wall four times the height of a man. Frantically, he felt the surface with his hands and discovered crevices large enough to use as footholds where the large stones met. Quickly making his decision, he climbed the wall not knowing what he would find on the other side.

CHAPTER 7

Jacob Sash had the motionless body of Eleanor Townsend slung over his right shoulder. She didn't weigh much, so he carried her through the damp tunnel with little effort. Her faint floral scent filled his narrow nostrils. He never understood why women wasted their time with such trivial things as perfume from the apothecary. If they only knew the ambitious things he spent *his* time on, they would readily cast aside their senseless trinkets and gossip to join him.

Sash was a part of something big, something which would guarantee the survival of the Commune indefinitely. But those in the Order could not fully execute their plan as long as the undesirables, like Eleanor Townsend, continued to interfere. He hated these undesirables with a passion. Their incessant need to meddle only made him more eager to destroy them.

Eleanor wasn't the first undesirable he had taken care of. There were many more, and he was sure there would still be more to come. Sash could remember each and every one of them. His first had been his undesirable parents. He hated everything about them and all they stood for.

* * *

Sash's parents said he was a fool for supporting the Order and their grand plans. His father had shouted at him, "You will destroy the Commune, not preserve it. Why can't you see that, Jacob?"

He became furious at his father's words and how his mother just stood there, silently agreeing. He wasn't a child anymore. He was sixteen and could make his own path. He didn't need his parents any longer. The Order understood the world they lived in. The Order understood what needed to be done. The Order understood him.

The anger and hatred Sash felt for years boiled to the surface, turning his face red. His parents would not listen to reason; they were the problem. They were the undesirables the Order told him about. He had to put a stop to them spreading their ignorance.

Sash reached next to the blazing fire and picked up the fireplace poker. Feeling the weight of the iron in his hand, he jabbed at an ashen log in the flames. Making his decision, he gripped the poker tightly with both hands and swung it. The sharp hook hit his father's skull with a crack. Sash watched as the light faded from his eyes. The man that had once been his father crumpled lifelessly to the floor.

"Jacob," his mother shrieked. "What have you done?"

He lunged toward her and thrust the poker into her soft abdomen. A cry of pain escaped her lips as she collapsed to her knees, her hands trying in vain to hold in the sudden rush of blood from her stomach. Tears were streaming down her face as she continued to wail in pain. He drew back the iron poker and thrust at her again. This time he aimed for her chest and pierced her heart. She fell silent as her life left her.

Sash went into his bedroom and removed the blankets from his bed. He went back out to the room where his parents lay slain and held the corners of the fabric in the fire until they caught. The bundle in his arms got hotter as the fire began to consume the fibers. He tossed one of the blankets into each room of the small house and let the flames spread to the furniture, walls, and wood floors. Sash left the house as it became engulfed in flames. He never looked back.

From that day on he abandoned the filthy name "Jacob" his parents gave him. From that day on, he would be called Sash.

* * *

Sash smiled as he recalled his transition into adulthood. He'd chosen his own path and proved how useful he could be to the Order. He had been doing this work ever since the day he walked away from the burning remnants of his past life. His technique had been polished over the years. He learned how to control his rage and do less conspicuous work. After all, he couldn't burn down every building he did a job in just to cover his tracks and make it look like an accident.

Some of his targets were not so lucky as to be killed. What awaited them was something worse. Eleanor Townsend was one such target. His usual sneer crept over his lips as he thought about the hell she would soon be trapped in. She hadn't screamed when he bagged her, though. *Pity*, he thought. Sash loved when they screamed.

He reached the end of the long dark tunnel. He stood before a thick steel door with a single, dim light flickering above his head. He made a fist and banged on the cold metal two times. He heard shuffling behind the door, and a strip of metal at eye-level slid away to reveal a small, rectangular window. A set of eyes masked behind tinted, round goggles peered out at him, surveying the load hoisted over his shoulder.

"I've got another one for processing," Sash said.

The metal strip slid back into place covering the tiny window. Sash heard the grinding sound of metal scraping against metal as the gears were engaged to unlock the door. It swung inward to grant him entrance.

CHAPTER 8

Travis kept his eyes downward as he chopped apples and tossed them into a large stockpot on the stove. He hated working in the Commune kitchen, but it was where the Elders had assigned him. When he turned thirteen in three days, he would finally be able to choose his own profession. He gave his sister's offer to work with her a lot of thought. It would not be as suffocating as it was in the kitchen. He would gladly trade the smell of simmering stews and baking bread for the earthy smell of the stables. He still hadn't made up his mind, but Jennie's offer was more enticing by the hour.

Travis thought he might have liked working in the kitchen if it weren't for the dociles at the opposite end of the room. They were enclosed in a row of small glass rooms. The blue-tinted glass partitions were unbreakable; no one could get in or out. Only one docile was kept in an enclosure at a time to prevent them from awakening their dormant pack instinct. This procedure was for the safety of the townspeople, but it did not put Travis at ease. For all the safety measures the Elders put in place, he could still see the dociles.

Travis knew the dociles were mindless creatures who didn't have the bloodlust of their violent kin, the lemerons. But every time he closed his eyes to sleep, he would see the lemerons in the forest beyond the wall dragging his mother away. Their gnarled hands gripped her arms as she struggled to break free. He would never forget his mother's desperate screams.

Each day during his shift in the kitchen, he would see the dociles through the blue glass. They looked no different from the lemerons. In his mind, they were the same. The dociles were a daily reminder of how his mother had been taken right in front of his eyes.

He tried to cheer himself up by thinking of how fortunate he was to not be on dish duty. The dociles performed menial tasks, such as washing dishes or doing laundry for the medical center. They were given simple repetitive activities which required no mental capacity, which was good, because they had none. All the same, someone still had to bring the dirty dishes to them and collect the clean ones. Travis felt glad his job of food preservation did not require him to go near the dociles.

"You look distracted." Madam Marie said, standing beside him as she cut carrots. "What's on your mind, my boy?" She put the kitchen knife down and searched his face for the answer.

"I've been thinking a lot about my thirteenth birthday and…"

"And you no longer want to work in the kitchens," Madam Marie interrupted.

She was very intuitive. Nothing ever got past her. She was the head of the kitchen, and supervised Travis and his coworkers. She had never married and had no children, but she had a soft spot for Travis. Madam Marie cared for him like a son and always seemed to know what he was thinking.

"Well," Travis said.

He was worried she would be disappointed if he no longer worked with her. He didn't want to let her down, but he longed for the opportunity to work where the dociles weren't around. He liked Madam Marie, but was miserable being around the dociles. He struggled to find the right words to communicate this to her, but nothing came to him. All he could manage to say was, "yes."

"I imagine it's because of your mother, rest her soul. I know how hard it can be having a constant reminder of the tragic loss of a loved one." Madam Marie gazed ahead, searching a horizon that wasn't there. She turned her attention back to Travis and said with sincerity, "Travis, you should choose a profession where you can feel your purpose in life being fulfilled. Choose a profession which makes you truly happy. You won't find that here."

Madam Marie had found the words Travis was searching for. He couldn't stay in the kitchens with the dociles. They were always staring blankly through their yellow eyes, always slowly moving their grey hands to complete their task. Not really alive, yet not really dead. Their presence was oppressive.

He decided that on his thirteenth birthday, he would choose a profession where he could be surrounded by life. He would work where he could breathe freely and never have to work alongside the half-dead dociles again. Travis wanted to work with his sister Jennie in the stables.

"Keep stirring the apples. You don't want to scorch the ones on the bottom." Madam Marie smiled to Travis.

"Thanks," Travis returned her smile.

While Travis stirred the apples in the pot, he listened to the idle conversation of the women nearby. He began daydreaming about what it would be like to help Jennie tend to the horses. Maybe she would let him ride one of the horses from time to time. He had only ridden a horse once, but the thrill of the magnificent beast transporting him stuck with him. It was one of the few memories he cherished. It was a joyful experience from a happy time in his life.

A loud bang startled him. Sash unceremoniously entered the large bright room. Travis stopped stirring and looked up. The women stopped as well and turned their attention to Sash's large figure standing in the doorway.

"The Elders have called an emergency Commune Council." Sash said in his gravelly voice. "Everyone is required to depart for the Sanctuary immediately."

Sash slipped away as quickly as he came. Everyone laid down their work and began making their way towards the door. Travis removed the apples from the heat so they wouldn't burn, and followed the group of women. They all moved out of the kitchens and down the hallway towards the Commune dining hall.

"An emergency Commune Council?" one of the women said. "I wonder what it could be about?"

"I hope it is not about *another* crop being lost to disease. We're already on strict rations as it is," another woman said.

"Oh, I hope you're right. I'm afraid we will starve if our farmers can't produce enough food. The growing season is almost over," said a third woman.

Travis was worried. Emergency Commune Councils were only held if something terrible had happened. Madam Marie, sensing Travis' tension, put a soft hand on his shoulder to steady him. As they crossed the town's main square, more people were coming out of buildings to join the ever-growing crowd. Travis felt uneasy, even with Madam Marie by his side, as they approached the double doors of the Sanctuary and entered the Commune Council chamber.

CHAPTER 9

The Commune Council chamber was a grand room with electric chandeliers hanging from the tall ornamental ceilings. It was filled with many rows of neatly arranged chairs to seat the entire Commune population. Opposite the entry stood a large platform, with a row of chairs facing out toward the gathering hall. The Elders and the Advisors were already seated on the platform, watching the townspeople gather.

Victor Glassman was one of the two Commune Elders. He was a proud man in his fifties, with grey hair matching his eyes. Victor seemed to relish the authority as an Elder, and he had an uncanny ability to command an audience. Travis found him to be intimidating, even though Victor was always polite when addressing the Commune.

Marlene Saunders, the Commune's other Elder, always looked stern and let her expressions do her communicating rather than speaking. Despite her youthful appearance, she was as old as Victor; maybe older, but no one knew for sure. Marlene's green eyes and long, blonde hair stood out in striking contrast to her pale complexion.

Travis scanned the room and spotted his sister, Jennie, sitting in a back corner next to her friend, Belle. He excused himself and left Madam Marie to make his way over to his sister. He slid into the empty chair next to her. Jennie and Belle were huddled together, deep in a muted discussion. They didn't look up when Travis joined them.

"…what other secrets…" and "…she seemed scared of something…" and "…need to go somewhere private to read it…" were all hushed phrases Travis could hear of their discussion. It was perplexing, and none of it made sense to him.

Belle leaned forward and stared at Travis with alarmed eyes, realizing he had joined their vacant corner. Jennie turned in her seat to face him. She looked concern, but she forced a smile to reassure him. Travis knew Jennie always tried to shield him from things she felt were hard to bear. It was part of her protective instinct, which had greatly increased since they lost their mother. Travis knew she meant well, but it made him feel like a child all the same.

"Hi Trav," she said, with forced optimism.

"Jennie, do you know what's going on? Why have they called us all here?" He asked.

"I wish I knew," Jennie answered, as her strained smile melted away. "Hush, now. People are starting to take their seats. We can talk later."

Travis heard Belle ask Jennie quietly, "How much do you think he heard? Can we trust him with this?"

Travis whispered into his sister's ear, "What were you two talking about?"

"Not here, not now. Later..." was all she said, looking forward to the podium.

The last of the people had entered the room and were now taking their seats, filling in the empty spaces around Travis, Jennie, and Belle. Elder Victor stood at the center of the podium, his face expressionless, and raised his hands to call for silence. A hush fell over the crowd as they all watched him expectantly. Travis could sense the others around him were just as apprehensive as he was.

"My fellow townspeople," Victor began, "you have all been called here today to join us for an emergency Commune Council. By the Founders' decree of emergency Council proceedings, we will forgo formal opening statements and procedures.

"I regret to inform you that one of our fellow Commune members, Mrs. Eleanor Townsend, has disappeared." A concerned murmur spread through the room. "We have testimony from Advisor Sash," Victor gestured to the man with no hair behind him, "that she was last seen at lunchtime walking towards the northern wall. As many of you know, this is also where her husband James was last seen before his disappearance a month ago. We can only assume that the grief of her husband's loss led Eleanor to search for him. Advisor Sash informed me he saw her leave the Commune through the small access gate. She was then accosted by a lemeron."

A woman in the crowd shrieked at the mere mention of a lemeron. The room began to buzz with chatter about the terrible news. Travis felt his face flush, and he began to tremble. It was shocking to learn Mrs. Townsend had suffered the same fate as his mother.

Victor waited for the room to fall quiet and he then continued. "Your Elders, Marlene and I, are concerned with the safety of our people. We ask that no one venture to the wall and by no means should anyone leave the safety of the Commune and enter the forest."

Travis touched his face and his fingers came away wet. He wiped his tear-soaked face with his sweater sleeve and turned to look at Jennie. He saw that she was shaking with the news. He felt sad for her, as Mrs. Townsend had been her favorite teacher in school. He studied his sister's face and saw her expression was not one of sadness or fear, but of anger. He had never seen his sister's face so cold and hard before.

Jennie looked furious; her piercing stare did not stray from the podium. Travis tried to follow her line of sight. As he attempted to decipher who Jennie was staring at so fiercely, something caught his eye which he didn't expect. Instead of looking concerned, as one might expect, Elder Marlene wore an expression of hatred and disgust. Marlene was boring a hole through the back of Victor's head with her eyes. Travis knew something was off. His fear dissolved into concern for both himself and Jennie.

CHAPTER 10

Jennie stormed out of the Sanctuary and down the steps with Travis and Belle on her heels. She had been a fool to believe the Elders would be honest with them. She *knew* Mrs. Townsend didn't just wander off outside the wall. Just before she disappeared, Mrs. Townsend was confronted in her classroom by none other than Jacob Sash, the supposed witness to her disappearance.

In the town square, Jennie spun around on her heel to face Belle and her brother. "We have been lied to. We need to go where we can talk safely. Follow me."

She turned and quickly walked through an alley by the school. She was being cautious by not taking her usual route in case someone might be following. After all, Jennie and Belle were the last ones to see Mrs. Townsend before Sash appeared in her classroom. He was a threat to them now. He might suspect that they wouldn't believe the so-called "testimony" given at the Commune Council.

The three of them continued to walk through hidden alleyways and narrow passages between buildings, careful to avoid the main paths. From the corner of her eye she saw three tall men standing like watchmen but when she looked in their direction, she realized they were just shirts hung on a line in a backyard to dry. She heard the creaking of a door opening in the narrow alley behind them and looked over her shoulder, still hurrying forward. The creaking door wasn't a door at all; only a shutter swinging freely in the wind on its rusty hinges.

Jennie's heart raced; she was jumpy and paranoid. She wasn't even sure if anyone even *was* following them but couldn't take that chance. They had to get the answers they needed, and the key to this was resting safely in the bag slung across her shoulder. She hurried through the apple orchard, weaving her way through the trees. When glancing back, she was relieved to see only Belle and Travis behind her.

They emerged from the apple trees and rushed down the sloping hill towards the brown, wooden barn. From the outside, it looked simple with its four walls and a pitched roof. There were no outwardly facing windows on the first floor, only two large doors on either end of the long building. The only windows to speak of were on the second floor above the two doors. They were giant square holes cut in the side of the building used to pull the hay and grain into the loft using the pulley hanging outside.

Jennie ran to the barn door and opened it just enough for the three of them to squeeze through and closed it promptly behind them, securing the latch from the inside. As she quickly walked the length of the barn, she checked each stall to ensure they were alone with the horses. She locked the door at the far end of the barn before walking back to Belle and Travis. She finally felt safe.

"This way," Jennie said leading them into her office.

She had repurposed the unused horse stall across from Misty's and turned it into an office. She had laid spare wood planks on the dirt floor and outfitted the space with a small table and two wooden chairs. She kept the horse tack neatly organized along the side wall; bridals and reins hanging from pegs, brushes in one bin, hoof picks in another. She knew exactly where everything was and could tell at a glance if something was out of place.

She pulled out the two chairs and invited Belle and Travis to sit. Jennie went to the corner and took an empty crate and placed it on its side, creating a makeshift stool. After sitting down, Jennie placed her bag on the table. Belle looked on with anxious anticipation while Travis had a confused look on his face. Jennie couldn't help but feel a combination of both of these emotions.

"Let's see it then," said Belle. "You can finally show me the pictures Mrs. Townsend presented in class."

It struck Jennie that Belle had missed the last class Mrs. Townsend would ever teach. It had been the most meaningful class Jennie had sat through in her school career. She sighed, extracted the old, leather-bound book, and placed it on the table.

"What's that? A book?" Travis scratched his head.

"This is why Mrs. Townsend disappeared," Jennie replied solemnly.

The old leather crackled as she opened the brittle cover. Jennie gingerly removed the pictures Mrs. Townsend had inserted between the pages. She showed Belle and Travis the photos spanning the two hundred years of the Commune's existence. She told them everything Mrs. Townsend had explained concerning them, about what they revealed, and about Elder Marlene being in every single one.

When she was finished, Belle and Travis sat staring at the faded color photos spread across the table surface. Their eyes were wide and mouths slightly open. No one knew what to say. Finally, Belle broke the silence.

"Hearing about it earlier stunned me. Seeing it takes it to a whole other level. Is this how everyone else reacted during class?"

"Pretty much. We were all speechless." Jennie said. "Then the bell rang for lunch just after Mrs. Townsend revealed it was Elder Marlene in every single photo. She is an Elder *and* a Founder. I still don't know how it's possible. How is it that she doesn't age? There are too many questions I will never be able to ask Mrs. Townsend,"

"The book might be able to give us some answers," Travis suggested. He cocked his head to the side, studying the book. "What is it, anyway?"

"I don't know," Jennie inserted the photos between the pages and lifting the book, "but it's really old from the looks of it."

Jennie examined the book she held delicately in her hands. The tan cover was made of smooth leather, dry and cracked with age. The vellum pages were a deep cream, discolored with time. The once black ink was now a light grey, having faded over the years.

Closing the book, Jennie ran her slender fingers over the front – there was something embossed in the leather. Specs of gold leaf clung in the grooves on the cover. The rest of it rubbed off long ago. Jennie could not make out what the design was, but as she traced it with her fingertips, she recognized a familiar shape. It was the outline of a horse.

Jennie reached into her bag and pulled out a sheet of blank paper and a pencil. She placed the paper on the cover of the book and rubbed the flat side of the graphite back and forth over the embossed cover.

"What are you doing?" Travis asked.

"There's something on the cover that I can't make out. I'm making a rubbing of it."

The three of them leaned in, peering at the image that materialized in front of them. The gentle back and forth motion of Jennie's hand was mesmerizing as subtle lines were revealed. When she stopped moving the pencil, they all leaned in even further to get a better look.

"What is it?" Belle asked.

Jennie lifted the paper and held it close to her eyes, tilting it to make out the details of the rubbing. "It's a horse, a rearing horse. It's surrounded by a circle made of some sort of… leaves?" Jennie slid it across the table so Belle and Travis could see it.

Belle squinted at the rubbing. "I don't understand what a horse with some leaves around it has to do with anything. Why would they take Mrs. Townsend away for that?"

"There might be something explaining what this symbol is and what it means inside the book," Jennie suggested.

"You said Mrs. Townsend got her information from the Secret Archives. So, this book must have come from there too. What if this horse engraving has something to do..." Belle stopped speaking abruptly. The color drained from her face.

The loft floorboards above them were creaking. Someone was moving up there. Jennie's stomach began to turn over. She forgot to check the loft. Fear clenched her body so firmly she felt as though she were suffocating. They were not alone.

CHAPTER 11

Jennie signaled with her hand to Travis, indicating that he should stay put. She crept across her office to the tack wall. She scanned the wall and picked out a riding crop – a sort of small whip – and a pitchfork with sharp tines. She beckoned Belle closer.

She gave Belle the pitchfork. "Take this and stand behind the base of the ladder to the loft. Keep out of sight." Jennie whispered. "I'm going up there."

With pleading eyes, Belle shook her head in protest. Jennie pretended not to see.

She leaned her head out of the opening to peer down the central aisle of the stable. When she felt confident the way was clear, she motioned for Belle to follow. The loose earth floor of the stable helped muffle their footsteps. When they reached the base of the ladder, Jennie signaled to Belle to move around behind it and stay out of sight. She pointed to herself then up towards the loft.

Jennie gripped the riding crop in one hand and the ladder in the other. She took a deep breath and began to climb. When she was about halfway up, she and paused, listening for movement overhead. She heard the faint rustling of hay in the front corner of the loft, just above her office. She continued climbing, her heart beating in her throat.

Her eyes were now just above the floor, so she could peer out across the loft. Her view to the far-right corner of the loft was obstructed by loose hay spread across the floor. She advanced another rung of the ladder. Her shoulders were now exposed, but her view was still obstructed by the stacked bales of hay towards the far end of the barn. It never occurred to her this could prove to be a useful hiding place for someone.

Jennie put the riding crop down in front of her and placed her hands flat on the wood floor. She used her arms to steady herself as her legs climbed another two rungs, then she brought her feet under her, knees tucked to her chest. She remained in the crouching position listening for what felt like hours, but it had only been a few minutes. She could no longer hear any movement, but she was certain whoever was up here with her was in the corner where she fixed her gaze. She wished in this moment she could see through the hay blocking her view.

Her heart was racing, and she could hear her speeding pulse in her ears. She stood and brushed feebly at the bits of hay that clung to her sweaty hands. She scooped up the riding crop and advanced. She wished she had the sharp metal pitchfork, but it would have been too loud and bulky coming up the ladder. The riding crop, with its small fold of hardened leather at the end of the two-foot stick, was her only protection now.

Jennie was careful to avoid the floorboards she knew creaked when walking on them. She gripped the riding crop with a shaking hand to steady herself and keep up her nerve. She heard a subtle movement ahead of her, and she stopped to listen. The sound was coming from behind a pile of hay bales just ahead of her to the left. She tiptoed forward and positioned herself so that she was standing with her back pressed against a stack of hay.

Jennie took a deep breath, trying to muster her courage and strength. She would find out who was hiding in the loft and what they were doing there. It unnerved her that all she had to defend herself was the little whip. It might not be much use against someone like Sash, but she had the element of surprise. Whoever it was behind the hay, she was ready for them.

Jennie rounded the corner with the riding crop raised high above her head. She froze, her eyes wide with surprise. *Who is this?* she thought. *I've never seen him before.*

There was no such thing as a stranger in the Commune; everyone knew everyone else. But this man was just that, a stranger. Jennie was staring into the face of a young man, approximately her age within a year or two. His piercing, bright green eyes stared back at her. Dark stubble covered his firmly set jaw. She could not gauge his height because he was sitting down, but she could tell he was lean and muscular. He was quite handsome.

She could have stared at him indefinitely, taking in his striking appearance, if it weren't for his outstretched hand pointing a sharp looking dagger directly at her. She saw the green sleeve covering his left arm was stained brown with dried blood. Her eyes darted back to his face again, not wanting to miss a change in his expression which might indicate if he were about to lunge. She noticed beads of sweat on his forehead, and he looked unusually pale. The two of them were in a stalemate, and neither of them dared to move.

Jennie finally found her voice and settled for the most direct questions. "Who are you? Where have you come from?" she demanded.

"My name is Ethan McAllister. I come from outside your wall," he replied, still wielding his dagger.

"That's impossible. There are no humans left beyond the wall. Now lower your weapon."

"Is that what you're made to believe here?" Ethan lowered his arm and placed the dagger in its sheath on his belt with strained effort.

"I will be asking the questions." Jennie snapped back. "Why are you in my stable?"

To her surprise, Ethan volunteered the information without hesitation. "I was in the woods on a scouting mission. My people received word that there was an unusual pattern of lemeron migration to the south. I was sent to investigate. I got caught in a storm and got lost. That's when one of the lemerons attacked me," he said, gesturing to his left arm with a tilt of his head. "I fled and ran into your wall. This was the first building I saw and I wanted to get out of the rain."

Jennie was struggling to accept this free-flowing information. She wondered if it might be a trick. Perhaps Sash had agents who could plant themselves amongst others to spy. Ethan began to cough violently. The effort drained him and he collapsed on his bed of hay. As she peered closer, his face looked even more flushed than it was before. His wretched condition helped to dispel her concerns and made his story believable. After witnessing the atrocious lie fed to the entire Commune by one of the Elders, she was inclined to believe this stranger over her own leaders.

Jennie's head spun with the realization that she and the people of the Commune had been lied to about more than just Mrs. Townsend. Ethan's earlier statement of "what you are *made* to believe" bothered her. His account of how he got here alluded to even more people living outside of the wall. The people of the Commune were always told that they were the only humans left; there was no one else beyond the wall. Yet here sat Ethan, living proof the teachings were wrong. The people of the Commune had been misled about everything.

CHAPTER 12

Ethan thought the girl might faint. Her face grew white as he explained why he was in the forest and how he found his way to her stable. She clearly had no idea there were other people living outside of their wall. He wondered what kind of place sheltered their people in ignorance such as this.

"Are you all right? You look pale. Maybe you should sit down," Ethan suggested.

She nodded and sank down on her knees, sitting on her heels. She still held the small whip in her hand, but now her grip was loose. Ethan could see she was attractive. Her auburn hair had been pulled gently back and tied behind her head. Her blue eyes were stern when she first rounded the corner, but they had softened while listening to him. They now were distant and gazed right through him, making him feel invisible.

"What's your name?"

"What?" she said startled, as if suddenly pulled out of a deep thought.

"Your name?" Ethan repeated.

"Oh," she said, her eyes now focusing on his. "Jennie."

"Jennie," he repeated. "It's nice to meet you. And who are your friends downstairs?" Seeing the alarm on her face, Ethan promptly added, "I heard people talking earlier, so I assume you're not alone."

Ethan watched her sit for a moment, apparently thinking about something. Then she shouted over her shoulder, "Belle, Travis, it's safe. Come up here. Put the things on the table back into my bag and bring it up with you." She paused then added, "And bring the medical kit on the shelf in my office."

Ethan noticed that she was staring at the dried blood on his sleeve. He watched as she scooted closer to him, reaching out to examine his left arm. She smelled faintly of apples.

"Take your tunic off, let me see how bad it is," she said.

He hesitated. "Can't you just roll up my sleeve?"

"I doubt it can be pulled up that far. I can always cut the sleeve off."

"And ruin a perfectly good tunic? I don't think so."

With his good arm, Ethan pushed himself up to a sitting position.

"It might be ruined already with all that blood and those holes."

After the exertion of climbing over the wall, his left arm was still too painful to use, so he awkwardly maneuvered the shirt over his head with his right arm. Pain ripped through his left shoulder with the effort, and he cringed, swearing softly under his breath. A cold autumn breeze blew in through the window causing him to shiver without his thick, warm tunic.

Although her touch had been soft, Ethan flinched with pain as Jennie examined the extent of his wounds.

"Bring a bucket of water, some rags, and a blanket," she called down below. "When did this happen?" she asked him.

Ethan peered into the sky through the open window of the barn. The clouds were streaked with color. He watched absently as bright purples, reds, and oranges blended into the deep blue of dusk. Soon the only light would be from the stars and the waning moon.

"Almost two nights ago, I think," Ethan said. "I might have lost track of the days."

"You've been up here for all this time?" Jennie asked astonished.

Ethan nodded.

"Did you even have anything to eat?"

"The thought of food made me nauseous. I came in here looking to rest," he told her.

The truth was he had hardly noticed the passage of time. He slipped in and out of consciousness while laying here on his bed of hay. Hunger had not come to him, only the need to sleep.

Sweat trickled down Ethan's forehead and he wiped it away with the back of his hand. He felt his energy draining away again as he rotated his body to prop his back against the hay bales behind him. Hay prickled his bare skin as he relaxed. His limbs became heavy and he let his arms sink to his side. The world faded away and he slipped out of consciousness.

CHAPTER 13

All Belle could hear from above was muffled talking. She couldn't make out any of the conversation taking place above her. She strained to make out the tone of the exchange. If it were Sash up there, she would've expected to hear screaming or shouting. Instead it almost sounded like a calm discussion is taking place.

She felt something was off. She imagined Sash overpowering Jennie. The talking she heard was probably Sash detailing the terrible things that would happen to her. He would make her disappear, never to be seen again. He was probably threatening Jennie's family and friends if she didn't tell him everything she knew about the Secret Archives.

It was unbearable just waiting to know what was going on. Belle was worried for her best friend and the desire to protect her was overwhelming. She was still standing where Jennie had indicated she should stay out of view – just inside one of the vacant stalls behind the loft ladder. If Jennie had to leave the loft in a hurry, Belle would be here ready to protect her.

The work she did in the morning at the solar farm left her hands raw and blistered. Wringing her grip around the wooden handle of the pitchfork only made it worse. It was a nervous attempt to convince herself this ordinary stable tool could become a weapon. If she could only grip it hard enough...

She wondered if Travis was feeling this same level of anxiety. It must be worse for him since he was told to stay put in Jennie's office. He probably couldn't hear anything.

Belle jumped and dropped the pitchfork with a clang when she heard Jennie shouting. *Looks like I didn't have a good grip after all*, she thought. Jennie's words had been clear. They were instructions for Belle and Travis.

She rushed over to the office and found Travis, still sitting at the table, his eyes wide with fear.

"Grab a bucket and fill it with water, quickly," She barked at Travis. "We need to get up there."

She scooped up the book, photos, and the paper with the horse rubbing. While placing the items in Jennie's bag, she made her way over to the tack wall. Scanning the shelf with her eyes for the medical kit, she wondered fearfully if Jennie was injured. She spotted it next to a pile of neatly folded rags. She grabbed the supplies and rags, and shoved them into the bag. Finding a stack of horse blankets, she took one from the top of the pile. *This will have to do*, she thought, and rushed out of Jennie's office. Travis was coming towards her with a bucket filled with water.

Belle slung Jennie's bag over her shoulder and motioned to Travis. "Here, trade with me." She offered him the blanket and took the water.

It troubled her why Jennie needed all of these supplies. She wondered if Sash hurt her and that's why she needed the medical kit. It was also strange that she wanted the materials given to them by Mrs. Townsend. Maybe it was an exchange: the items for Jennie's life.

They made their way over to the ladder. Standing at the base, they stared up through the access hole cut in the loft floor. All they could see from there were the wooden beams which supported the roof running. Belle took a deep breath.

"Let's go," she said, trying to keep her voice steady for Travis.

With difficulty, she climbed the ladder with her free hand, holding the water bucket at her side with the other. The wire handle of the metal bucket cut into her fresh blisters making her grimace with pain. She tried to adjust her grip on the handle by bending her wrist, but water sloshed over the top of the bucket, soaking her pants. No matter how she tried to hold the bucket, the handle still pressed cruelly into her blisters.

With relief, Belle finally reached the top. She stepped out onto the floor and pressed her sore hands together, trying to ease the pain. Travis was climbing up right behind her, and fumbled with the blanket as he reached the loft.

"Where are you?" Belle called out to Jennie.

"Over here," Jennie responded, her voice coming from Belle's right.

Belle picked up the water bucket, and led Travis through the middle of the tall stacks of hay. She thought how incredible it was that Jennie had piled all of this hay by herself. It was quite physical work and she was so petite. Belle continued to walk towards the end of the loft. She felt a breeze tousle her curls as she neared the window.

She reached the end of the barn and halted. The sight before her was not at all what she expected. Jennie was kneeling next to an unconscious young man; his shirt was off for some reason. As she stepped closer, she saw his left arm was bloodied, and Jennie was examining it.

Belle let out a sigh of relief that Jennie wasn't hurt and hadn't needed the medical kit for herself – it was for this man. She felt a pang of guilt because she was relieved the man was injured instead of Jennie. She didn't want anyone to be hurt at all.

Belle set the water bucket down and gave the sack to Jennie. "Who is he?" she asked.

"A stranger named Ethan," Jennie responded, "He's from beyond the wall."

Belle heard Travis gasp. She had forgotten he was right behind her.

"From beyond the wall?" Belle repeated. Saying the words didn't make them feel any less strange. Everyone in the Commune was told repeatedly that there was no one left outside of their settlement. Yet here this man was, proof this teaching was wrong. "What else have they lied to us about?" she muttered.

Jennie looked up and met her eye, "That is the question we need to answer."

CHAPTER 14

"Ethan may be able to help us answer some of our questions," Jennie said.

"How did he get so badly injured?" Belle asked.

"He said he was caught in that awful storm the other night and got disoriented in the forest," Jennie began, as an explanation. "He claims he was attacked by a lemeron. The way he described it, he barely got away alive."

Both women watched as Travis collapsed to his knees. He was shaking and tears were streaming down his cheeks. Jennie went to Travis, knelt down, and held his shoulders firmly in her hands. She looked into his eyes.

"We can't help our mother now, nor can we bring her back," Jennie said softly. "But we can help save this man. I need your help to do that. Will you, Travis?"

Travis nodded, wiping his tears away with his sleeve.

Jennie stood and helped Travis to his feet. "Come sit over here by me. You can hold the medical kit and pass me the instruments as I call them out."

Ethan's left arm had five deep puncture wounds. Jennie surmised they were from the lemeron's fingers when it grabbed him. Yellow pus was oozing from each injury. A foul odor hung in the air around his arm causing Jennie to scrunch her nose. His bare chest was gently rising and falling with his deep breaths. He was unconscious, but he was alive.

"He's fighting off an infection. We need to thoroughly clean the wounds and stitch them closed."

"How do you know how to do all this?" Travis asked.

"I have to know for when the horses get injured in the fields. The farmers are careful with them, but sometimes a buried root gets ripped out of the ground by a plow and nicks the horses. If the wound is severe enough, I have to stitch it closed."

"I've heard the farmers say you are more focused than some of the doctors in the Commune." Belle said proudly.

Jennie took a clean rag, dipped it in the water, and wrung it out. She began to clean the wounds in his left arm. When the cloth became too blood-soaked, she would rinse it in the bucket, squeezing out the excess water. She continued in this manner until all the pus and dried blood was cleaned away. His arm looked better, but there was still more work to be done.

The last light of day was now gone. Jennie took a lantern hanging from a nearby post and lit it with matches from her bag. In the flickering light she could see large, purple bruises on his bicep surrounding the puncture wounds.

"Travis, in the medical kit you will find a bottle of alcohol and cotton. Pass me both of those please," Jennie instructed.

Travis did as she instructed, and she dabbed the wounds with alcohol-soaked cotton to sterilize each injury.

"I need the curved needle, suture thread, and scissors," she said to Travis, who passed the items to her with a trembling hand.

Using the alcohol, she sterilized the instruments. When she pierced Ethan's skin, she felt his muscles tense. Jennie stopped and searched his face for signs that he was regaining consciousness. If he awoke now, it would make her work more difficult. In her experience, it was easier to stitch up a subdued horse than a fully aware horse who could become frantic. Jennie imagined people were the same.

"Travis, put the riding crop in his mouth so he can bite down on it if he wakes up," Jennie had seen this done when she observed procedures in the medical clinic. There, they used wooden rods and not whips.

Travis opened Ethan's mouth and put the crop between his perfectly straight teeth. "Like this?"

"Perfect," Jennie nodded at him with approval.

She was able to finish stitching up each of the five wounds without Ethan waking up. She reached over and took a roll of gauze out of the medical kit and wrapped it around his arm a few times to ensure his injuries remained clean. She tied the gauze off and cut the end. Leaning back, she admired her handiwork.

"Wow, you're fast," Belle said, from the corner.

Jennie slowly let her mind relax now that Ethan's arm was cleaned and stitched. She removed the riding crop from Ethan's mouth and the rag from his forehead. With another moistened rag, she wiped the sweat away from his face and his upper body. Jennie couldn't help but notice how handsome he was. The flickering light from the lantern accentuated how toned Ethan's exposed torso was. Absentmindedly, she let her eyes trace the contours of his lean muscles. Her eyes wandered from his toned shoulders and chest down to his muscular abdomen. Suddenly, she felt a flutter in her stomach and turned away to pack up her medical supplies.

"I know that look," Belle gave a coy smile. "You're taken with him."

"Don't be silly, I don't even know him," Jennie answered, blushing. She found the warm horse blanket and covered Ethan with it, so only his handsome face was visible.

"But you didn't deny it," Belle teased.

CHAPTER 15

Sash entered the tower from the third floor of the Sanctuary and began to climb the stairs. He stepped onto the little landing before a small arched wooden door with large ornate metal hinges. He lifted his large fist and pounded twice on the solid wood. Moments later, the door opened. Victor stood before him, still dressed in the dark purple robes of the Elders.

"Come in and close the door behind you," Victor said flatly.

Sash entered the sprawling room with its lavish furnishings. He followed Victor across the stone floor covered with red silk rugs in elaborate designs. They sat in cushioned chairs angled toward a roaring fireplace with a carved stone surround and mantle. Sash loved fire. It was so cleansing and reminded him of his rebirth into adulthood.

"Well done today," Sash said, "those undesirables actually believed every word you said at the emergency Council."

"That may be so," Victor said, "but we cannot become over confident. There may yet be those who doubt us."

Sash let a knowing sneer spread across his thin lips, "What do you need me to do?"

The two men sat silently in front of the fireplace, their shadows dancing on the wall behind them. Sash was observing Victor closely, trying to read any thoughts which might be revealed by his facial expressions. He knew it was in vain, though, Victor never projected what he was thinking on his face.

Victor finally spoke, "When you saw Eleanor Townsend leaving the Sanctuary this morning, she likely took something after accessing the Secret Archives. It's very possible the information she gathered was shared. This could be very dangerous for us, for all of us in the Order."

His grey eyes were now transfixed on Sash, the orange flickering of the fire reflected brightly in them. "Find out who she was last in contact with - her co-workers, her students, the damned person who served her lunch. I want to know if any of them are acting suspiciously, but be discrete about it. Report back to me once you find out who we need to deal with next."

Sash grinned, "It would be my pleasure."

He stood up and left the room.

CHAPTER 16

Sitting at the carved wooden desk in his study, Victor finished writing the death certificate for Eleanor Townsend. She was a nuisance, and he was glad to be rid of her. He signed off on the document making it official. He leaned back in his oversized leather chair and reveled in his work. *She got what was coming to her*, he thought. *She won't be able to recruit anyone else in her current state.* She, of course, wasn't dead. Victor thought that would be too good a fate for her. Yes, an eternity of living hell was much better suited for defiant people such as her.

The Order had readily sanctioned the processing of Eleanor Townsend. It hadn't been hard to get the authorization since Victor was the head of the Order and had a very compelling case. Their most reliable footman, Jacob Sash, had been following Eleanor ever since they had eliminated her husband, James. Victor knew it was only a matter of time before she entered the Secret Archives, searching for answers to her husband's disappearance. The Order feared the release of information stored in the Secret Archives and would go to any length to silence those who threatened to do so.

He rose from his chair, picked up the small lantern on his desk, and collected the death certificate. He left his dwelling and descended the spiral staircase. He enjoyed the coldness of the stone walls around him. It made him feel invigorated. As he stepped out into the third floor of the Sanctuary, he was not surprised to see that it was deserted at this late hour.

The little lantern cast a small glow in front of him, giving him just enough light to see by. He walked down the long corridor, reaching more stairs at the end. He continued to make his way down until he reached a door labeled "Lower Level – Records."

Victor extracted a key from a pocket in his purple robes – only the Elders had access to the Commune records – and he unlocked the door. Marlene never came down here, so she would have no idea how Victor had transformed the records room. Before his innovation, he had to manually file all of the birth, death, and marriage certificates, the annual crop yield ledgers, and all of the other Commune documentation. It was tedious work, and he disdained it.

He previously requested an assistant to do this filing for him. The matter was put to a vote during one of the Commune Councils. His request was denied. He could still picture the chamber filled with people, the majority with their hands raised, voting against him. Each one was an undesirable in his eyes from that day on. Systematically, he had been getting rid of them. He no longer had to do the mundane task of filing documents, thanks to his ingenuity.

Victor had instructed the Order to install the unbreakable blue glass separating each row of filing cabinets. Every row held a specific type of record, and there were hundreds of rows. All he had to do now was go to the end of the appropriate row, open a little door at waist height, and insert the paper. From there a docile would take the document and file it away.

The dociles worked out to be perfect for Victor in his grand plan. He now had just over a hundred dociles doing menial tasks down here. The records department was only the start - with its success, the Order had started to plan for other docile work assignments. Their ability to complete mindlessly repetitive tasks made them perfect for plowing the fields, harvesting the crops, boiling the stews.

The dociles were well suited for these types of jobs, and most importantly they were passive. The lemerons had an unending hunger for living flesh, whereas the dociles did not. Dociles only needed to eat about once a month, so there would be plenty of food for all of the remaining humans in the Commune. Soon, dociles would replace the farmers, the cooks, and every other type of job that did not require higher cognitive faculties, all the work that living people – the undesirables - currently did. The undesirables were nothing more than a drain on resources.

The Commune could then re-route the electricity. Dociles could see exceptionally well in the dark. In contrast to humans, they could hardly see at all in daytime due to how their cloudy eyes processed the light. The Commune would no longer need to route electricity to where the dociles would be working. This meant Victor could finally get electricity in his quarters at the tower. What was the point of holding such a high position of power if he had to live like a common undesirable?

It always cheered Victor up to think about his perfect little world, where the only humans would be the Order members and those by special right – the scientists, the doctors, the inventors. He walked down the long records room and came to a stop by the row of filing cabinets labeled "Death Certificates." He opened the little door, inserted Eleanor Townsend's death certificate, and watched a grey-skinned figure with yellow eyes slowly materialize from the far end of the row.

"Hello, James," Victor said, for his own amusement. Dociles did not have names, nor did they have memories, but Victor remembered who each docile had been when they were still humans. "Your wife, Eleanor, will be joining you down here soon."

Victor smiled triumphantly as the docile picked up the document to be filed, turned and vanished into the darkness.

CHAPTER 17

The amber glow of morning spilled through the gaps in the green leaves above him, creating vertical stripes of light all around. He was looking for something, but he couldn't remember what. He could see the trees moving, but he couldn't hear the leaves rustling in the gentle breeze.

"Travis," a far-off voice was calling to him. It familiar, but he couldn't place who it belonged to. "Travis. Over here."

He looked down at his hands and saw he was now holding a cloth sack. He knew he had to find something to fill it with. He still couldn't remember what he was searching for though.

"Travis, I found some," the voice said.

He picked up his foot to begin walking, but the forest blurred around him. Within one step he had already traveled the distance and reached the owner of the voice. He looked down at a girl, hunched over and filling the same kind of sack he held. He bent down next to her to see what she was collecting. When he saw the girl's face he recognized his sister, Jennie, only she looked much younger.

She was gathering mushrooms from the forest floor. Damp soil clung to her fingers. With each mushroom she picked, he got a whiff of its earthy scent.

Jennie smiled at him and said teasingly, "Your bag isn't going to fill itself."

Travis reached out for an enormous mushroom by his foot, but his hand couldn't reach it. The more he stretched his arm, the further away it became. He felt like he was being pulled into the sky by a thread attached to his back. He was floating now, light and carefree.

He heard a woman scream. The thread snapped, and he plummeted to the forest floor, crushing the mushroom he had longed to pick only a moment ago. Another scream, only this time it was louder and closer. He looked in the direction of the sound. A woman ran toward him. She was shouting something, but he couldn't understand what she was saying. The desperation in her voice ripped through his entire being. Her fear alarmed him. She kept running toward him, but she never got any closer.

Travis was being carried over Jennie's shoulder, still looking back at the woman. He wanted to do something to help her. He stretched out his arm, but just like the mushroom, he could not bridge the distance between them. Desperation took hold. He stiffened his arm, hoping to further his reach, but it didn't help.

Jennie was carrying him away from her. No. This was wrong. The woman was getting too far away. He began kicking his legs. He had to get to her, but his sister was taking him in the wrong direction. He couldn't leave this woman. He had to help her. Why didn't Jennie understand this?

The golden glow of the forest changed to red as flames sprouted from the ground. The green leaves on the branches browned and crumbled away as the trees turned black. He felt terror as the peaceful forest transformed into an inferno. Travis never took his eyes off the screaming woman. Fire surrounded her. All of a sudden, the flames became grey and took the shape of monsters. The woman was surrounded by lemerons, their grimy fingers grabbing at her.

Travis watched as the lemerons took hold of her and dragged her away. She struggled against their grip and kept screaming. He reached out to her, extending his arm, hoping she could grab his hand. But she was too far away now, her screams becoming faint cries in the distance.

He could finally hear what she was trying to say to him. She was crying out for him to run. She wanted him to be safe. She was his mother.

* * *

Travis woke up with a start in a pool of sweat. He sat up and hugged his legs to his chest, burying his face in his knees. His body trembled as he let himself cry.

After a while, Travis wiped his tears and looked around. He was back in his house, in his bed, with his warm blanket. He could not remember how he got here or when he fell asleep. All he could remember was how the lemerons took his mother and how he would never be able to eat mushrooms again.

CHAPTER 18

Jennie was busy working in the kitchen of their cottage home when Travis entered from the hall. She had a small table cover laid out and was piling bread, jams, dried meats, and canned fruits and vegetables in the center of it. She brought the corners in and tied the bundle together with a rope, creating a makeshift sack.

"What time is it?" Travis asked, rubbing his bloodshot eyes.

"Probably somewhere around three in the morning. You should get some sleep, you only had about two hours," Jennie said.

"When did we get back? I don't remember coming home," Travis said.

"You went downstairs while I was cleaning up in the loft. When I went in my office to put the supplies back, I found you asleep at the table. I carried you home." Jennie wrote a note as she explained, and left it on the table. "We got back to the house around one in the morning, I'd say."

"Did you get any sleep?" Travis asked Jennie.

"No. There is too much to do," she replied.

"I can help," Travis offered. He wanted to help out, but he also wanted to sleep.

"You can," Jennie said, "but only after you get some sleep. You can meet me in the stable after you get up."

"But I..." Travis started to protest, but stopped when he realized how tired he was. The previous day had been long and draining.

"Make sure Father reads the note when he wakes. I've written that we were working at the stable late due to Misty's pregnancy." Jennie picked up the bundle of food.

"Don't mention anything to him, or anyone, about Ethan. There has never been an outsider in the Commune before, and we don't know how people will react if they find out. Remember, we were all taught the only remaining humans are within the Commune. Father included. Ethan is a direct contradiction to that."

"Don't worry, I won't say anything," Travis said, and he meant it. What could he say about Ethan? He didn't know anything about him other than the fact that he faced a lemeron and lived.

Jennie smiled and tousled Travis' already disheveled hair. Travis watched her walk out of the house through the kitchen door and disappear into the night. He walked back into the bedroom and lay down in his bed. Pulling his blanket up to his chin, he closed his eyes and drifted off into a deep, peaceful sleep. He did not dream.

CHAPTER 19

Ethan woke to find himself alone. He gazed out of the window as he tried to collect his thoughts. He remembered Jennie and her friends being there, and Jennie looking at his wounds. His bandaged arm was still painful. He hoped his fever had finally broken since he was no longer suffering from a cold sweat. He suspected it had been Jennie who patched him up. He would have to remember to ask when he saw her next. At least, he hoped he would see her again.

The fruit trees growing in the little meadow next to the stable were so still at this hour. The wind had ceased, but an autumn chill hung in the air, which made him glad for the blanket clutched around his shoulders. He had no desire to be anywhere else as he sat there watching the fog form slowly across the silent ground below. Everything had a blue pallor to it from the light of the moon above.

He was happy to see the slender figure of a girl roughly his age making her way through the apple trees. *It must be Jennie*, he thought. She was carrying a large sack over her shoulder. It looked heavy, but she managed it with ease. As she got closer, he could make out her oval face – it was indeed Jennie. Ethan felt a strange sensation as he watched her that he had never felt before. His legs were tingling and his stomach fluttered.

Ethan heard her climbing the ladder, and watched as she made her way over to where he was sitting. It was quite late, or rather early, for her to be coming back to the stables. Having not been awake when she left, he had no idea how much time had passed, but he found he was glad for the company regardless of the time.

"I didn't expect you back so soon. Shouldn't you be sleeping?" Ethan asked.

"I couldn't sleep tonight even if I wanted to," Jennie said. "I'm usually up in a couple of hours anyway. I thought you'd still be sleeping."

Ethan watched as she settled down in front of him. She took the large bundle and set it between them. Unfastening the knot in the rope, she let the fabric fall away revealing a wide assortment of food and a canteen of water.

"I thought you might be hungry. You're looking much better now, so the infection must be under control."

Ethan didn't know what to say; she was so kind and thoughtful. "Thank you," was all he could manage to get out.

"I brought you bread and jam, fruits and vegetables, some dried meat. I hope there is at least something here you like."

"It's all wonderful." Ethan picked up a piece of dried meat.

After tasting the first bite, he realized just how hungry he was. He hadn't had anything to eat or drink in days, and he was very happy to have such an assortment. The dried meat tasted delicious and was coated in spices to enhance the flavor. He took the canteen, unscrewed the top, and put it to his chapped lips. The cool water felt like new life, rejuvenating him as he drank.

They sat together silently as he ate. Jennie's soft features were accentuated in the light of the moon. He noticed she was looking him up and down as if she were trying to read or understand him. Ethan became aware that he was not wearing his tunic and only had the horse blanket to cover his upper body, which he pulled tighter around his shoulders. No wonder he felt a little chilly; he was missing a vital piece of clothing.

Jennie broke the silence. "Your tunic is hanging just over there," she pointed to a makeshift clothesline above his bed of hay. "I was able to wash most of the blood out and mend the holes. It should be dry in the morning. Things take longer to dry in the cold air."

Ethan looked to where she had been pointing and saw the dim outline of his tunic. "Thank you," he said. "You have been very kind to me."

"You're welcome. It's not every day that we have strangers here to visit," Jennie said with a teasing smile. Her expression turned somber. "All my life, I've been taught that we are the only humans left in the world, and that our Commune is the last remaining refuge of humankind. Your presence here directly contradicts that. I need to understand more about the outside world and why we are taught this lie."

"Well, I may not have the answer as to why you and your people were misled," Ethan broke off a piece of bread and dipping it in the jam. "But I can tell you that it's not a very friendly place out there beyond the wall."

Jennie closed her eyes and took a deep breath. "I need to know if I can trust you. My teacher, Mrs. Townsend, was trying to reveal the truth to us, and then suddenly disappeared under suspicious circumstances. Your being here exposes the lie that we are the only humans left. This means you are in the same danger she was in." She paused as if to let her message sink in. "You are no safer inside this wall than you were outside with the lemeron who attacked you."

Jennie confirmed his suspicions that there were people here who would keep the truth silenced at all costs. He wondered how many of them there were and what they would do if they found him. Jennie didn't seem to be one of them; she had taken care of him, patched up his wounds, brought him food, and even cleaned his stained and dirty tunic. Ethan trusted her, and in turn, he wanted her to trust him.

"If what you say is true, I won't be able to stay long," Ethan said regretfully, not wanting to think about leaving Jennie behind. He had just met her, but he enjoyed spending time with her and didn't want that to come to an end. "During my time here, I will do whatever I can to help you find the answers you seek."

Jennie reached into her shoulder bag and extracted an old leather book. "I think this is the reason why Mrs. Townsend disappeared. You may be able to help me make sense of it all."

Ethan leaned in as Jennie showed him a series of pictures that she took out from between the book's pages. She explained the twenty-five-year intervals since the Commune's founding roughly two hundred years ago. In each photo, she pointed to a woman with blond hair and green eyes. It was indeed strange to see her in every image, never aging. Ethan peered closer at one of the photos of the woman where other people didn't partially obstruct her from view.

"She looks familiar," Ethan said distantly, trying to place her. "She looks like…" he paused and furrowed his brow as it came to him. "…my mother."

CHAPTER 20

"Your mother?" Jennie exclaimed, with disbelief. "How can that be?"

"I don't know," Ethan said. Jennie saw emotional pain registering on his face. "My mother abandoned me in the woods when I was only a baby." He paused, took a deep breath, and then continued, "A ranger found me, and took me in. When I grew old enough to understand, he told me how I was found and gave me the only thing that I had in my possession at the time."

Jennie watched as Ethan reached into his back pocket and took out a folded piece of heavy paper. He held it in his hand for a moment, then outstretched his arm offering it to Jennie. Curious, she took it and began to unfold it. It was a colored photo with worn creases running horizontally and vertically down the center dividing the image into four sections. The color was all but gone in the creases, probably from Ethan folding and unfolding the picture so many times.

Jennie's hand shot to her mouth. "Marlene."

Holding the photo in the light of the moon, Jennie could see a beautiful woman with strong features, blond hair, and green eyes. She was smiling and looked genuinely happy. In her arms, she was holding a happy baby with cheerful green eyes and a tuft of dark hair on its head. She glanced from the image to look at Ethan and saw he had the same green eyes. It had never occurred to her that Marlene might have a family. Marlene rarely spoke and Jennie realized she didn't know anything about her.

Jennie could see that this was hard on Ethan. His eyes now held pain instead of the blissful happiness captured in the photo. She didn't know which was worse: being abandoned and never knowing your mother or having a loving mother who was taken away by lemerons. All Ethan had left of his mother was a photo; at least Jennie had memories of her mother.

She suddenly felt hopeful for Ethan. His mother is Marlene and an Elder in the Commune. She could reunite the two of them after just shy of two decades of separation. Jennie knew that there was no hope of ever seeing her own mother again, but helping Ethan find his mother encouraged her.

"This woman, your mother, she is one of our two Commune Elders. I can take you to her," Jennie said, with excitement in her voice.

"No," Ethan said sternly.

She noticed that when he spoke, his voice trembled slightly with pain - or was it anger? Jennie slumped and her arms fell to her side. She was sure he would say "yes." She thought he would be glad to have an opportunity to meet his mother. He must have noticed the shock on her face, because he spoke again.

"Read the back," Ethan said.

Jennie turned the photo over in her hand and noticed that there was something written there. The penmanship was neat and fluid. The ink was faded and hard to make out. Jennie held the thick paper closer to her eyes, squinting in the dim light.

My dearest son Ethan,

You have brought me so much happiness in your short life and I wish our time together could have been longer. The world in which we live in is no longer safe and I am unable to keep you from the growing dangers. I can only hope that you are found by someone who will care for you as much as I do.

Someday when you are older, you may feel the need to try and find me. Please don't come looking for me. This is for your own protection. All I want for you is to be safe, and you will not be safe with me, not now, not ever. I don't expect you to understand, but just know that you will always be in my heart.

With all my love,

Mother

When Jennie looked up, she saw sorrow in Ethan's eyes. Empathy overwhelmed her, and tears came to her eyes. She tried to imagine why Marlene would leave Ethan alone in the woods where the lemerons lurked. How could the woods be safer than here within the walls of the Commune? Jennie wondered if Marlene hadn't yet come to the Commune, but then she recalled how Marlene had been in every Commune photograph for two hundred years. Nothing made sense to her.

"My mother doesn't want to see me. She made it very clear in her letter to me. I have read that message countless times throughout my life, and the meaning of the message is always the same. There is no other way to interpret it."

"But she says she did it to keep you safe."

"How is it safe out there with the lemerons? How could she possibly think that leaving a baby on the ground in the middle of the forest would be safe?" Ethan raised his voice. "She left me to die out there. She doesn't care about me."

Jennie reached out and touched Ethan's hand to console him.

"I'm sorry. I shouldn't have lost my temper like that."

He took her hand in his and gently squeezed, acknowledging the gesture. A jolt of electricity shot through her arm, and she felt the fluttering again in her stomach. Ethan met her eyes, and his cheeks turned a soft pink color.

Was he experiencing the same electrified touch that she was? She blushed. Jennie tipped her head down and removed her hand from his. Slightly embarrassed, yet not sure why, she tried consoling him with her words instead.

"I know what it feels like to lose your mother. Lemerons killed my mother four years ago. My brother, Travis, and I watched as they dragged her into the forest. There was nothing we could do. The last thing I remember is her crying out for us to run and to save ourselves." Jennie paused, trying to keep her tears from spilling over. It had been years since she had cried, and she couldn't start now, especially not in front of Ethan. "If there is anything that I can do to help, please let me know."

"I didn't realize that you have also suffered so much." Ethan shook his head as if to clear away any assumptions he had about Jennie. "It was selfish of me to think that you wouldn't understand. People usually don't, but you seem different."

A sheepish smile came across Jennie's face, and she knew for certain she was blushing. The fluttering in her stomach was stronger than ever.

CHAPTER 21

The air was cold outside, and the fog felt like icy death. It burned his esophagus and lungs as Sash inhaled the damp chill. The way the frigid air cut through his innermost organs made him feel invigorated and powerful. The air warmed inside him, and he exhaled through his mouth so he could see his breath hanging in front of him. He could manipulate how the air behaved simply by breathing.

He stood waiting in a shadowy space between two buildings that flanked the town square. The only light was from the bright moon that hung in the sky overhead. The moonlight cast long shadows all around the square in front of him. There were no sounds to be heard at that late hour, except for the distant hooting of an owl.

To Sash's left, he saw a shadow move quickly across the far side of the square. The shadow came to a stop next to a figure that emerged from a building's portico. He smirked. This is what he had been waiting for: a meeting between undesirables. He hated them. They were stupid enough to have a private discussion out in the open. The darkness couldn't protect them. Sash was the darkness, and he was everywhere.

Sash backed up and turned around. He made his way through the back alleys and reached the far side of the square where the two figures stood. He heard the hushed voices of a male and female, but he couldn't make out any words. It didn't matter to him; he had no desire to hear what an undesirable said. At the mere thought of hearing a conversation between them, Sash spat on the ground.

He picked up a large rock and palmed it in his hand. He tossed it gently to feel its weight. It was heavy with jagged edges. He spun around the corner and lunged at the two undesirables. He swung his arm, and the rock collided with the woman's head with a loud crack. Her scream echoed through vacant streets. Blood splattered his face and the nearby wall as she collapsed to the ground. The man ran frantically to get away from him.

Sash could outrun nearly any man – something Victor found exceptionally useful – but he permitted the other undesirable to get away. *I will get you next time*, he thought. He had one of them and that was enough for now. The man would tell his co-conspirators of the attack and spread the fear that Sash thrived on.

Kneeling down next to the woman, he could see she was still breathing. Blood seeped from a gash on her forehead, and pooled on the ground near her face. Pleased with his work, Sash extracted a black sack from his back pocket. He opened it and slid it over the woman's head and cinched it closed around her neck.

Her short, thick body was as heavy as a large man, but Sash picked her up with ease. He carelessly lifted her onto his shoulder and disappeared through the alley from which he came.

CHAPTER 22

"I think you misunderstand the meaning of discretion." Victor yelled. He gestured with an open hand to the body that lay on the floor. "Look at her. She is making a bloody mess everywhere. We can't just go around leaving traces of violent attacks in the street. What will happen when the sun comes up, and the people see the blood splattered everywhere?"

Sash just shrugged. Victor looked at him with disgust. "You need to think these things through. It's bad enough you let one get away. What if word spreads about the attack?"

"I hope it does," Sash shot back. "The undesirables will be too afraid to even look at each other, let alone plan anything."

Victor rubbed his hand down his face in exasperation. "This will be a setback, but until I say so, no more attacks. I need you to do information gathering *only*." He extracted a white handkerchief from his robes and tossed it to Sash. "Clean yourself up."

Sash took the cloth and wiped his face. He was irritated with Victor and how he could be so narrow-minded sometimes. The Commune was overflowing with undesirables who wasted resources. The Order would give them a new purpose as dociles and bring about a new era of prosperity. Sitting around listening to these undesirables as part of "information gathering" was abhorrent to Sash. His face screwed up in disgust as he thought about it.

"Since the day I met you when you were still a boy, I have always thought of you as the son I never had," Victor walked to the window. His voice had recovered its calm quality. "You know that I would never have you do anything which didn't benefit the Order and our goal. This may not be the approach you want to take, but we must think of the big picture. Nothing like this has ever been attempted, and we must be secretive. The people cannot begin to suspect anything, or else our work will be in jeopardy." Victor turned to face Sash. "Patience is our ally."

Sash sighed. He hated waiting. He wanted to take action. The Order had been talking about this plan for the last seventeen years and slowly executing it. Sash supposed taking time with things was a good idea, as it didn't draw the attention of the people – the undesirables included. Only recently, once things accelerated, did some of the undesirables start to take note. Undesirables like Eleanor Townsend.

"All right," Sash said finally. "I'll be more careful. But, if I see the need to take care of a problem, I will. You have to agree we will still encounter trouble from the undesirables."

"Fine, but don't take any actions like this," Victor gestured again to the body, "for at least a week. We need to let things calm down first. Until then, just see what information you can find out."

"Fair enough," Sash tossed the now red cloth back to Victor. Despite his feelings, he would do it for his true family – the Order.

"Take her down for processing, then clean up the mess you left outside," Victor ordered, looking at his bloody handkerchief with distaste.

Sash nodded and picked up the body. As he was leaving, he heard Victor say to him "And Sash, remember, information gathering only."

CHAPTER 23

The tunnel was dark, as usual, and the sound of dripping water echoed throughout the long expanse. Sash's shoulder began to ache from the weight of his latest victim. He continued forward and grunted from the fatigue in his shoulder and arm. *Damn, what has this woman been eating?* Sash thought as he trudged through the darkness. His back felt wet; he wasn't sure if it was from his sweat or her blood.

A small point of light appeared as the tunnel curved to the right. He was nearly there. He banged on the reinforced steel door twice in his usual fashion then waited. After a brief moment, the small window slid open. Sash just grunted and shifted his body so the latest delivery was visible. The opening slid shut and the metal gears of the lock disengaged. The door creaked as it swung inward, and Sash stepped inside.

Sash's pupils were dilated from being in the dark tunnel, and his eyes strained momentarily in the brightness of the sterile room. The temperature was artificially cold, and the air was dry. The white walls reflected the light making it seem even brighter. The room had a bitter stench of chemicals, making his eyes burn. He was sure this must be why the processor always wore those tinted goggles.

"Where do you want her, Goggles?" Sash asked. He'd never cared to learn the man's real name.

The room was large enough to house two steel tables evenly placed in the center. They were long and narrow, just the right size for a body. To his left was a small door leading to Goggles' office with a glass window between the two rooms. Beneath the window was a row of cabinets and a counter with laboratory instruments and vials strewn across the disorganized surface. Directly across from Sash was another reinforced steel door identical to the one through which he had just entered. Sash had never been through that way, but he didn't need to ask what was behind it. He knew.

Lining the right wall was a series of pressurized drawers. Sash had previously seen Goggles open one and slide out a metal bed-like slab about the size of the tables in the room. At the time, Goggles had placed the body of a man who failed processing on the metal slab. He used a string to attach a slip of paper with a number on it to one of the man's toes. The drawer slid back into the wall, and the man was forgotten as the small door closed again.

"Put her on the table over there," Goggles said in his nasal voice.

Sash obliged, glad to be rid of his heavy load. He watched as Goggles donned a pair of rubber gloves and moved over to the woman. He removed the black sack from her head. He shook his head as he examined her injuries. He made a few clicking sounds with his tongue and looked at Sash.

"Her skull seems to be cracked, and she is bleeding profusely from this laceration. She's still alive, but barely. The probability she will survive processing is very low," Goggles said, removing his gloves. "Next time try to bring me a subject that is not severely injured."

"Just do what you can," Sash said indifferently. "Either way, my problem is solved."

* * *

Sash returned above ground with a bucket in hand. He went to the fountain that dominated the center of the town square. It had three carved horses in the middle, rearing up on their hind legs with their backs touching each other. From their open mouths, a steady stream of water poured out into the stone pool below.

Sash looked in the water. Round coins of various sizes blanketed the bottom of the fountain. He never understood why people would just throw their money away in the water. The people in the Commune were given a certain amount of money each month, and the coins were traded for goods and supplies. Sash would never waste his money on stupid gestures and useless items. All the more reason why they were called undesirables, their senseless behavior was not something the Order wanted in the Commune.

Noticing the sky was getting lighter, Sash broke away from his thoughts and carried on with his work. He filled his bucket with water from the fountain and made his way over to the blood-spattered wall. As he tossed the water at the wall, the red ran down toward the ground. After two trips to the fountain and back, the wall was clean.

He focused his attention on the pool of blood on the ground. He tossed more water on the red puddle and watched it turn pink and disappear between the stone pavers covering the ground. All it took was a few trips to refill his bucket, and he washed away the evidence of the attack.

His thoughts turned to the man who got away. Sash wanted desperately to make him pay for fleeing. Anger flooded him as he thought about the man who was too cowardly to show his face. He closed his eyes and imagined his hands wrapped around the man's throat, squeezing the pitiful life from him. His upper lip twitched, and he gnashed his teeth in anger. He didn't know who the man was, but Sash would be watching. He knew the signs to look for, and he was sure he would find this coward.

The sky was now turning a light-yellow color as the sun began to rise. Soon the square would be filled with people and undesirables. Sash couldn't bear the thought of being surrounded by those fools. He threw the empty bucket down an alleyway and heard a loud clang as it crashed against something stacked up on the ground. The violent act didn't make him feel at ease. Instead he felt rage building up inside him. Sash turned down one of the alleys and headed toward his house to sleep. He didn't think he could make it a week without doing what he did best. He couldn't go that long without ridding the Commune of more undesirables.

CHAPTER 24

Warm light touched Jennie's face, and she could see a pink tinted glow through her closed eyelids. Her eyes fluttered open to see the rising sun through the window. Disoriented, she took in her surroundings. The wooden rafters overhead and the familiar sweet smell of hay greeted her. Despite sleeping next to an open window in the middle of autumn, a horse blanket kept her warm – although she had no memory of how it got there.

Hesitantly, she pushed herself into a seated position. She yawned and stretched her arms out to either side to open up her shoulders. *How long have I been sleeping?* she wondered. Looking around, she could see that she was alone in the loft. Ethan was not there, and his tunic was no longer hanging to dry. Had he gotten dressed and left? It made her sad to think that he might have departed without saying goodbye. She noticed that her bag was still there with the book and the food she had brought the night before. That was a good sign.

Jennie stood up and walked toward the ladder in the middle of the loft. When she got closer, she heard voices and laughing from below. Curious, she climbed down and found Ethan and Travis feeding carrots to the horses. Relief flooded her that Ethan hadn't left and her heart warmed. She smiled at the sight of them holding their offerings out on a flat hand while a horse sucked the carrot up using its lips. Travis and Ethan were both having fun.

Ethan noticed her standing there and said to her brightly, "Good morning. The horses really love these carrots."

"Do you have horses where you come from?" Jennie asked, enjoying his enthusiasm.

"No. We live in houses high up in the trees, so we can't really keep any livestock," Ethan replied. "But we do have a lot of birds."

Jennie laughed as she imagined a horse living in a house built in a tree. "I can see how birds would be a little easier to manage up there."

"We already took care of all the horses while you were sleeping," Travis said, pride in his voice. "And I brought hot coffee."

"You are amazing, little brother of mine." Jennie tousled his hair. "Now, take me to this coffee."

They made their way to Jennie's office toward the front of the stable. Jennie saw that Travis had brought a complete breakfast: coffee, muffins, sausage, hard-boiled eggs, and even juice.

"Where did you get all this?"

"I stopped by the kitchens on my way over," Travis replied. "I thought I would tell Madam Marie I've made my decision. I will be working in the stables starting tomorrow when I turn thirteen. But she wasn't there. I guess she hadn't come in yet."

"That's great news. You're already doing wonderfully. I can see that the horses love you and your carrots from the kitchen."

They all settled in and had their breakfast. The first sip of coffee was invigorating to Jennie, and the food gave her the energy she needed to take on the day. Travis told her all about how he and Ethan took care of the horses that morning. Apparently, Ethan was timid at first, never having been around horses, but he got the hang of it pretty quickly.

"Just like taking care of the birds, just bigger and with four legs," Ethan teased.

When they finished eating, Jennie changed Ethan's bandages, and they all went into the loft and sat on the floor near the window. She felt elated. She was with Ethan again, her little brother seemed happy, and Belle would be joining them shortly. They were finally able to have a moment where they could find out what was inside the book Mrs. Townsend took from the Secret Archives. They had agreed to wait until they were all together to read it. Whatever they discovered within the yellow pages would certainly merit discussion.

Jennie looked across at Ethan and caught his bright green eyes looking at her. She felt a tingling in her body as he smiled at her. It pleased her to see that he was doing better and was recovering from the infection which had plagued his arm. His face had color, and he no longer had dark circles under his eyes.

Belle entered the loft and interrupted Jennie's thoughts. She came over and sat next to Jennie, out of breath. "Sorry I'm late. I heard some disturbing news this morning."

"What news?" Jennie asked. They all looked at her with anticipation.

"There was an attack last night, and Madam Marie has gone missing."

"Madam Marie?" Travis asked in disbelief.

That would explain why Madam Marie was not there when Travis went to the kitchens this morning. Jennie frowned at the thought.

"Where did you hear this, Belle?" Jennie asked.

"I overheard it from a couple of people I work with at the solar farm," Belle replied. "They seemed incredibly nervous about it and were barely speaking above a whisper. I had to strain to hear what they were saying, but it was unmistakable."

"We need to get to the bottom of this," Jennie said with determination. "This book may give us some answers."

CHAPTER 25

Jennie laid the book down on a small wooden crate she brought up to the loft to use as a makeshift table. Jennie glanced around at Belle, Travis, and Ethan; they were all leaning forward with anticipation. She opened the front cover of the book. It made a soft crinkling sound as the dry leather flexed. Jennie was close enough to the book that a faint, musty smell greeted her nose.

"Here we go," she said. She scooted forward so her crossed legs touched the wooden crate. The page contained faded, handwritten words in a neat script. She read aloud for the benefit of the others.

"Day 1 —

I decided to start this journal to document what is happening. When we are all dead, maybe someone will find this and be able to learn from our mistakes.

The nights are growing longer, and our party is becoming uneasy. There are only forty-two of us left, and our numbers are slowly diminishing. No one has heeded my recommendation that we need to move on and leave the flatlands which are being overrun by lemerons. Our leader, Jeremy, scoffed at my words, saying a woman knows nothing of such things. He is headstrong, stubborn, and foolish. We have never gotten along, and he has always resented me - for what I do not know.

I know in my heart this place is no longer safe.

Day 2 —

This evening, some of the party was out in the fields gathering corn. The night was closing in, and so were the lemerons. Back in camp we heard terrible cries, but the corn was so tall we could not see where those poor, screaming people were. We gathered our weapons and went searching for our friends.

We searched the expansive field for hours, but it was too late when we found them. The lemerons were already devouring their flesh. Nothing remained but a bloody pile of bones. I fell ill at the very sight. I can still taste the vomit in my mouth.

One of the creatures looked up at me with a red stained face and gleaming, yellow eyes. It rushed at me, and I was afraid. Before I would become its next victim, I swung my sickle. The curved blade cut through some corn stalks and the lemeron's neck. I watched as its head fell from its shoulders and rolled on the ground. The headless body fell forward and clumpy brown blood – I could only assume it was blood – spilled on the ground.

I heard another sound nearby and ran toward it. I reached there just in time to see a lemeron rip a chunk of flesh out of Jeremy's arm with its teeth. He fell to his knees and let out another scream. It was terrible. I used my sickle to attack this lemeron and was able to remove its head, the same as the other one. I find this to be the most effective way to destroy the monsters.

I was shaking with fear, but I helped Jeremy up, and we went back to the camp where our doctor wrapped his wound with rags. As I write this account, I know that I will find no sleep tonight.

Day3 —

We had a small remembrance ceremony for those who were killed yesterday. The people are uneasy and never take their eyes off the cornfield. They are afraid of what may be lurking there, hidden from our sight.

Despite the attack, Jeremy says this place is safe, and we must remain. I am afraid he will get us all killed if he continues with this. He nearly got himself killed. Jeremy barely survived this attack, and he looks like walking death. His skin is slowly being drained of its color.

I suspect he is becoming delusional from his injury.

Day 4 —

Jeremy is no longer able to speak. When he tries to open his mouth, only a harsh sound comes out. Even though we have had our differences, I do not want to see anyone else die. I fear for the worst.

Day 5 —

I was wrong. Jeremy is not dying. It is something far worse. His eyes have developed a cloudy film, and he no longer seems to recognize any of us. Everyone is uneasy, but no one wants to acknowledge what is happening to Jeremy.

Day 6 —

I burned the cornfield today. If the lemerons are approaching, I want to see them coming. The party has started to look to me for guidance, and I will not let us sit here waiting for our inevitable doom. I have instructed everyone to gather as much food as they can carry and leave their personal possessions behind. We will abandon this forsaken place in two days' time.

Day 7 —

Jeremy attacked me. Although it wasn't really him - it was only his body. Jeremy died the moment that monster bit him. He has become one of them now. He has become a lemeron.

I was caught off guard when he attacked me. I heard slow shuffling footsteps behind me, and turned around to see Jeremy, now turned lemeron. He – no, it – charged toward me, trying to grab me with his boney hands. Fortunately, I was able to sidestep its advance. I grabbed a nearby ax and buried it into its skull. I suppose the old saying holds true for us in an ironic way: we buried the hatchet.

I will never be caught without a weapon on my person again."

Horrified, Jennie stopped reading. She swallowed hard and looked up at the others. Belle's face was white and she was biting her fingernails. Travis had his legs pulled into his chest resting his chin on his knees, his eyes were wide with terror. Ethan sat still with a rigid posture.

"So, this Jeremy person turned into a lemeron after being bitten by one?" Belle's voice trembled as she spoke.

Ethan responded, "It seems so. I didn't think that could happen. Then again, I have never heard of anyone surviving an attack, the victims are always..."

Ethan's voice trailed off as he looked towards Travis. Travis was shaking, his face buried in his knees, and he was sobbing. Ethan looked at Jenny apologetically. Their mother being taken by lemerons was still hard on Travis and Jennie. They never truly knew what happened to her, but a detailed story of what happens to lemeron victims was more than unsettling.

"I think that's enough for now," Jennie placed a small slip of paper between the pages to mark their place and closed the book. "How about we get some more of that coffee?"

CHAPTER 26

The coffee warmed Belle from the inside. She was thankful to be within the Commune walls, safe from the lemerons that could be lurking in the surrounding forest. The horrifying account in the book made Belle shudder. It made her realize they weren't just dangerous, but their condition could be spread through a bite. She felt nauseous as she thought of the people being devoured by lemerons in the cornfield. Would she have the courage to defend herself against lemerons like the woman in the book did? She hoped she would never have to find out.

No one spoke as they sat around the table in Jennie's office. Jennie was tracing the wood grain of the table with her finger. Belle noticed Ethan was watching Jennie with curious interest. She wondered if there might be something between them. From what she could determine, Jennie seemed pretty smitten with Ethan as well.

Travis sighed heavily and broke the silence that hung in the air. "I'm sorry I got so upset earlier. I just…" his voice cracked. "It's hard hearing about the lemerons attacking someone."

"It's okay, Trav," Jennie offered a sympathetic smile.

"Let's get back to that book," Travis choked out. "There's something your teacher wanted you to know, so there must be more."

They gulped their coffee and made their way to the loft and sat down. Jennie opened the book to where she placed the slip of paper to mark her place. She cleared her throat and began to read aloud again.

"Day 8 —

Today we depart. We will no longer find safety in these flat plains. The thick forests and hills to the north will give us the protection we seek.

Everyone is carrying with them blankets and large quantities of food and water. Following my instruction, every man, woman, and child was also given some sort of weapon or sharp tool to defend themselves. I can't bear to lose any more of my friends. With Jeremy's death, there are only thirty-six of us left in the party.

Day 10 —

Our path so far has been easy, and we have not encountered any lemerons. The people are optimistic about finding a new home. They have begun talking about what it would be like to live in safety. I have to admit the thought of not having to constantly look over your shoulder wondering if you will be attacked is appealing. I must remain realistic though; these dreams may not ever come to pass.

Day 14 —

Today we were fortunate to find an abandoned wagon and horses. Perhaps things truly are looking up. We even found crates of food. Everyone was happy to be able to set his or her things on the wagon and travel burden free. We have decided we will all take turns riding in the wagon in groups of ten. This will help us keep up our strength and our spirits.

Day 18 —

It has been ten days since we left the cornfield and things are going well so far. The days are getting colder, but we are prepared with our blankets and warm clothing. We are covering a good amount of ground, but we are still in the flatlands. I long to see the hills which await us to the north. The optimism of the party remains high.

Day 37 —

The days are dragging along with our feet. The blisters from our shoes have now turned into hardened calluses. It has begun to snow, and I cannot feel my fingers in the cold.

Day 41 —

Our good fortune ran out. We were attacked in the early hours of the morning when it was still dark. The lookout fell asleep and never saw the lemerons approaching. It was a violent struggle. The party fought bravely, but we lost thirteen of our friends. Only twenty-three of us survived.

At least the lemerons do not care for animals, and we still have our horses.

Day 72 —

Our horses have grown weak, and we lost two more of our members to sickness. I am comforted they did not perish at the hands of the lemerons.

Day 83 —

We have run out of food. There is little to scavenge as the winter is upon us and the vegetation is dead. The outlook, is bleak and the party has little enthusiasm.

Day 86 —

We had to release the horses today. They are too weak and can no longer pull the wagon. They will be better off on their own finding grass buried beneath the snow to eat.

Some of our party members have been able to hunt for wild game. The meat tastes delicious after surviving on dried fruits and spoiled corn for so long. Things might be looking up for us now that our stomachs are full.

Day 103 —

We stumbled upon a small encampment of about fifty people in the gentle hills. There are not many trees around, but it is refreshing to see other people. They have welcomed us, and invited us to stay with them. There are proper cabins and fires here. It is so warm and inviting.

Day 157 —

We have been here about a month and a half, and we have all integrated nicely together. Their leader, Eric, and I have decided we should act as one community. We are stronger this way, and have a greater chance of survival. Our people get along very well with theirs, and some have even formed bonds.

Even Eric and I have grown close. I see in him the better part of myself, and I feel I can open up to him. I wonder what the future holds for us. Look at me, I sound like a schoolgirl. This is what humanity should be about: building friendships and finding love.

Day 163 —

We have been attacked again, only this time not by lemerons. Cruel people rode through our small settlement on horses and started attacking us. They stole food, clothing, and supplies. The attack was unexpected. and several of our people were killed.

I cannot believe the lack of humanity these people have. The state of the world we live in now does not mean we can act violently towards each other. We should all be coming together to fight our common foe, the lemerons.

Day 167 —

I am losing my faith in humanity. These aggressive people have attacked us again and taken more of our supplies. It is no longer safe here. Eric and I have communicated to our people that we will leave at dawn. We will carry on with my party's original plan and continue to travel north towards the safety of the forest."

Belle interrupted Jennie's reading. "Why would the people attack each other? Why wouldn't they want to help one another out? As she said in the book, her and Eric's people were stronger when they worked together."

Ethan responded, "The group of people who attacked them wanted their supplies." He paused then added, "Cruelty always comes to the surface when people are only interested in their own survival."

Jennie didn't say anything nor did she begin reading again. Belle saw she looked thoughtful; she seemed to be taking in Ethan's words. Something in Ethan's tone made Belle think he knew quite a bit about this concept of cruelty towards other people. Was he on the giving or receiving end of this cruelty?

CHAPTER 27

Belle changed the topic back to the contents of the book, "Maybe we will find out more about this group of cruel people in the next entries."

Jennie nodded and began reading again.

"Day 170 —

The attackers have not ceased. We abandoning the encampment and moving north. These people are barbaric and will cause our downfall if we do not protect ourselves. We cannot outrun them, so we must overpower them.

Eric disagrees with me. He feels fighting them will not solve anything. He wants to try reasoning with them even after they have already killed more than a dozen of our people. Eric is such a compassionate person, but I wonder if it blinds him at times.

Day 172 —

Eric went out searching for these barbarians to reason with them, and he has not yet returned. We have been in the same temporary camp waiting for him for two days now. We are vulnerable here and must keep moving if we are to remain alive. I fear for Eric. His extended absence has me sick with worry. I do not want to lose him.

Day 173 —

Eric has been returned to us, but he is dead. His feet were tied with rope, looped around his horse's neck. The barbarians sent the horse back to our camp, dragging Eric's body behind. They slashed his throat and scrawled a message on a paper pinned to his coat which reads 'you all will be next'.

My hands are shaking as I write this. No more, this has to stop."

Jennie stopped reading and spoke, "The paper is stained with small droplets, and some of the ink has run together. She must have been crying."

"That poor woman, I can't even imagine what that must have been like. Her pain must have been overwhelming," Belle said. "She finally found some small piece of happiness, and those barbarians destroyed it. How can people kill each other?"

Jennie frowned, "It's happening here too, cruel people killing others. Mrs. Townsend could attest to that if she were still here."

Belle thought of Sash and knew Jennie was right. She let Jennie continue reading.

"Day 175 —

The barbarians attacked us again, only this time we were ready for them. We fought back with a passion for survival which seemed to stun them. Many of them were injured and fled, but I killed one, and I was glad to take my revenge for Eric's murder.

I sank my curved blade deep into the man's chest. His dark eyes were wide and fixed on mine as he coughed up blood. I watched as the life left his eyes and his body went limp.

I took a human life. I am no better than this man. Nothing I do can bring Eric back to me. I truly am a monster.

Day 180 —

I wake from dreams where I see Eric with his throat slashed and then the face of the man I killed. He was a barbarian, but he was still a man. I feel like I am losing myself. I have become hardened and am not the stubborn yet light-hearted woman I once was.

How can I possibly lead my people now? I feel just as barbaric as those people who attacked us and murdered Eric.

Day ? —

I can no longer count the days. I don't know how long it's been since Eric was killed, but I know many moons have passed. I wish Eric were still here with me. I will never be whole again, I will never love again, and I will never feel alive again...

So many have died since we originally set out on our journey. I can't recall exactly when, but we had more lemeron attacks since my last entry. Our group keeps growing with newfound refugees. It then shrinks when some of us are killed by the lemerons. It seems that death is destined to follow me wherever I go.

I am cursed after all, so it makes sense that any good things that come to me cannot last. My people don't know of my curse, and I dare not write it down. If they find out, they will probably want to kill me. That is what people do when they are afraid – they kill each other. People will kill each other for anything it seems: fear, hunger, survival, cruelty, and even revenge. Must I live this endless life with the guilt of causing so much death and pain?"

Jennie stopped reading abruptly.

"Did she say endless life?" Belle asked. She shook her head as if it could not be possible. *But could it be possible?* She thought about the photos from the Secret Archives. It was the only thing that would make sense. "Is this Marlene's journal?"

"If so, I don't think we will find out from the journal," Jennie said regretfully. "The rest of the pages have been torn out."

CHAPTER 28

"You need to get your attack dog under control," said the gruff voice of Isaac Fenske, sitting across the table from Victor.

The interior room of the Sanctuary was dark and cold with no windows and no fireplace. The only light came from two small oil lamps placed in the middle of the wooden table.

Victor sat at the head of the table and could see the outlines of everyone sitting around the small room. He could not gauge facial expressions in the dim setting, but he could determine by the tone in Isaac's voice that he was in a challenging mood. Victor's face turned hot with aggravation. He was an Elder and the leader of the Order, and he would not be talked down to by anyone. Let alone someone like Isaac Fenske.

"Sash has done valuable work for us and has been a dedicated member of the Order for nearly twenty years," Victor retorted. "He has addressed the issue of the undesirables in the Commune more efficiently than – "

"And made a huge mess of it too," Isaac cut in. "He's reckless. And look, he doesn't even care to be here for the Order meeting."

"I will thank you not to interrupt me," Victor said sharply. "As it so happens, Sash is out there right now doing valuable work for us. We have a serious problem. Information has been leaked from the Secret Archives and he is finding out who knows about it. I don't think I need to remind you what will happen if this information becomes common knowledge," Victor finished with a warning tone.

"If I recall correctly, the information leaked because of your beloved Sash." Isaac snorted with indignation. "If it weren't for his crass way of handling James Townsend, we wouldn't still be cleaning up this mess."

"That's right," someone near Victor said. "His wife was motivated to spread our secrets to as many people as she could."

"She was trying to sabotage our cause by exposing what we are doing," said someone farther down the table.

"We know that she showed images from the Secret Archives to her whole class."

"Enough." Victor slammed his hand on the table. "Eleanor's students are all fools. They were too confused by the photos to even make any sense out of them. Her students are not a concern to us. Neither is Sash. As sanctioned by the Order, Sash promptly took care of Eleanor, and she will no longer be a problem."

He switched on his most influential public speaking voice. "I am filled with disgust as I sit here and listen to all of you speak so poorly about another member of the Order. Did we not all take the same oath? Are we not a group with a common interest? Our Order is stronger than a family. We are powerful. We each offer a unique skill set to further advance our grand plan."

He saw heads nodding in agreement with his words. "I refuse to hear of any more negative talk about Sash or any other member of the Order. When we start tearing each other apart, then we will have failed at our task. We will have failed each other."

Victor finished his speech by placing emphasis on each of his final words so they would sink in. He knew this would finally shut up that nuisance Isaac. Isaac enjoyed destroying those he felt threatened by, but he would never go against the common interest of the Order. Victor had successfully reminded him that attacking, verbally or otherwise, a member of the Order was going against the grand plan.

"Now, let us get back to why we are all gathered here." Victor leaned in and clasped his hands together on the table.

CHAPTER 29

Marlene sat on a gold cushioned stool and gazed out of her bedroom window in the tower. The room was adorned with heavy red drapes emblazoned with a pattern of gold leaves and flowers. It was a cozy space. She had her plush bed, wardrobe, writing desk, and a comfortable place to sit by the fire. The sun-bleached tapestries hanging on the walls were her favorite feature of the room. What once depicted vibrant, colorful scenes had now faded into muted memories. The time worn threads were much like her, a mere shadow of what used to be.

The glass looked like water poured over a smooth surface, a river frozen in time. The rippled effect gently distorted the scenes of life playing out below. Marlene reached out and ran her fingers over the glass, tracing the outlines of people mingling near the fountain in the middle of the square. The glass was cold to her touch. Marlene felt like this glass, as though she was forever suspended in time.

It was tiring never to age, to always be the same. She had lived the duration of many lifetimes, but she never had the luxury of aging. Her fingers found an elderly couple sitting on the edge of the fountain, holding hands and laughing with each other as they watched what Marlene assumed to be their grandchildren play. She touched the glass longingly. The simple pleasure of growing old with someone she loved would never be hers. It made no difference now even if she could age, because the man she loved was long gone.

She thought of her son, as she often did, and wondered if he was still alive. Was he better off out there instead of here? Sighing, she stood and walked over to a tall wardrobe.

The ornate wooden doors creaked as she opened them slowly. Her purple Elder's robes hung neatly inside. Standing on the tips of her toes, she reached the top shelf and used her fingertips to ease a large wooden box forward. When she had a solid grip on it, she pulled the box down and placed it on her bed.

Marlene sat on the bed next to the wooden chest and ran her hand along the top of it. The familiar shape of the rearing horse with leaves encircling it comforted her. In a time long ago, this symbol was widely used. People employed it as a silent means to communicate their dissent against those who oppressed them. Secret meeting locations, messages, and even tomes bore this rearing horse. This was the symbol of liberation and it was time she revived its use.

Marlene lifted the lid of the box and saw the relics of her earlier life. Most of the items contained within were older than the Commune itself and held special significance to her. Her eyes fell on a sharp piece of curved metal with a wooden handle. Her sickle. This simple farming tool had saved her life all those years ago. She closed her eyes and gently shook her head, as if to dislodge the memory from her mind.

She continued her visual search, scanning over a dried flower in a glass bottle, a leather belt with loops and pouches, and an old, battered canteen. Her eyes fell upon an iron rod. She reached into the box to extract it.

She felt the weight of the artifact in her hands as she examined it. The handle was made of a piece of coiled metal that provided a sturdy grip. The other end was flattened and molded into a circular brand about four inches in diameter. It was the inverse of the symbol burned onto the lid of her box. She looked at the metal that depicted a mirror image of the horse standing on its hind legs with the circle of connected leaves around it.

Long ago, people would brand their homes with this symbol to show their loyalty to the truth. The time had come for Marlene to reawaken its meaning, the meaning that was lost due to the passage of time and forbidden teachings. With the branding tool in hand, she walked over to the roaring fireplace in the corner. She held the end of the brand in the fire and watched as the black metal slowly began to glow red. She felt this transformation reflected her passion to fight for the truth. The drive that had been buried within her for so long revived and burned with the fury of the hottest flames.

Marlene removed the glowing metal from the fire and moved back over to the window. She pressed the symbol into the wood at the base of the glass. The sizzle of the hot metal searing an imprint into the wood was like music to her.

CHAPTER 30

Jennie hurried across the town square, not wanting to waste any time before getting back to the stables. They had come up with a plan to have Belle and Travis get more information about Madam Marie's disappearance.

Belle was going to try and get more information from the two men she overheard talking earlier this morning at the solar farm. Since Travis turned thirteen tomorrow, today was the last day he had to work in the kitchens. They decided to make the most of it and see what he could find out there.

Ethan, of course, could not be seen in the town, so he was still back in the stable. They had all agreed to meet in the loft that evening after Belle and Travis had finished with their afternoon work shifts to report what they were able to find out.

Jennie entered a small apothecary shop at the corner of the square. As the door opened, a silver bell chimed. The sound was swallowed up by the stuffy space. Jennie loved the smell inside the shop. It had a thick, earthy aroma perfumed with the sweetness of fragrant dried herbs. She stepped up to the wooden counter spanning the width of the shop. It had stacks of blank paper and piles of pre-cut strands of string. Floor to ceiling cabinets with hundreds of square drawers lined the wall behind the counter. Each drawer had a little label, yellowed with time.

After hearing the bell, a hunched man made his way through a door next to the cabinets. He had thinning grey hair and a receding hairline. He peered over the rim of his glasses to see better, and they slipped so far down his large nose Jennie was concerned they might fall off entirely.

When the man recognized Jennie, a large toothy grin spread across his face, exaggerating the fine lines around his eyes.

"Hello, my dear Jennie," he said happily. "To what do I owe the pleasure?"

"Hello, Uncle Albert," Jennie said smiling. He wasn't her real uncle. She didn't have any aunts or uncles, but Uncle Albert was close enough to be family. He was always there for her when she needed him, and he treated her like a daughter. "I need to pick up some more supplies." She extracted a list from her bag and placed it on the counter.

Uncle Albert took the list and pushed his glasses up his nose. He skimmed through the list and mumbled things such as "yes," "of course," and "indeed" to himself while nodding. It was always captivating for Jennie to watch as he worked.

He opened a small drawer, scooped a precise amount of dried herb or roots, piled it neatly inside one of the papers, twisted it, and tied it off expertly with a string from the pile. All of this he did with one, fluid motion. He then slid the tied bundles down the counter and repeated the whole process.

While he prepared her order, Uncle Albert asked her "You seem disheartened today, my dear. What is bothering you?"

The perception of this man never ceased to amaze Jennie. She hesitated a moment, then decided to tell him. "Someone I know has been attacked by lemerons." Jennie thought it best not to mention Ethan.

Uncle Albert stopped scooping some dried mint leaves and turned to face her. "I assume you mean your teacher, Mrs. Townsend?" There was something in his voice that betrayed bitterness. "Or perhaps your brother's friend in the kitchen, Madam Marie?"

Jennie was taken aback and didn't know what to say. No announcement had been made about Madam Marie yet. How could he have known about her?

"Don't you believe that rubbish for a moment," Uncle Albert said, no longer able to disguise the anger in his voice. "They were not attacked by lemerons, nor did they just decide to wander off on their own accord." His gentle eyes were worried, and he lowered his voice to a whisper as he continued, "You must be very careful about these things. Something terrible has happened to them both, but it was not the lemerons."

"But how do you –" Jennie began.

"It is best not to converse here," Uncle Albert interrupted. "There is a time and place for such discussions. There are others who can be trusted, other Truth Seekers. These disappearances are no mere accidents or coincidences. The group which stands against us is slowly reducing our numbers."

This sudden flow of candid information made Jennie's head spin. She leaned on the counter to steady herself. She had never heard about any of this before. Truth Seekers, and a group that opposes them?

Thinking back to the last time she saw Mrs. Townsend she recalled Jacob Sash was there. After that, no one saw her again. Jennie felt the bottom of her stomach drop as she realized the danger she and Belle were in. They had been the last ones to have contact with Mrs. Townsend. Sash might figure out she gave them information. There was a strong possibility Sash was in this group working against the Truth Seekers, and he might come looking for her and Belle.

Jennie cleared her throat and asked in a shaky voice. "How do I know who I can trust?"

"Unless they are introduced to you by someone you *can* trust, trust no one," Uncle Albert frowned. "Especially if they approach you on their own."

Jennie nodded uncertainly.

"I will arrange for you to meet a fellow Truth Seeker. Come see me this evening and I will introduce you." Uncle

Albert's face softened. "Until then, do not trouble your mind with these things. I hate to see you look so worried."

Uncle Albert finished preparing her order and smiled at her encouragingly. "No charge today, Jennie."

Jennie thanked Uncle Albert. Until she knew more about these "Truth Seekers," and this other group set to destroy them, she would keep Ethan a secret. She left the shop and crossed the square heading in the direction from where she came. As she hurried along, she wondered if Belle and Travis had found anything out. The events in the apothecary shop had her thoughts racing, and she couldn't wait to tell the others.

CHAPTER 31

The little corner in the loft was comfortable and felt like a second home now. Jennie brought pillows, blankets, and small stools from her family's cottage to make the space more livable. She was glad to make it cozy for Ethan since he couldn't leave for fear of being spotted. That would surely cause trouble and draw Sash's attention. Would Sash drag her away if he discovered she had been harboring an outsider? Jennie didn't want to find out.

Jennie reached the loft and saw Ethan sitting on a stool. He was studying the rubbing Jennie had made from the cover of Marlene's journal. She noticed he furrowed his brow as he studied the image of the rearing horse. The intensity on his face made her wonder if he had seen the image before. Perhaps he could help them determine what significance, if any, the symbol had. As she approached where Ethan sat, she reached into her bag and took out an apple. "Think fast." Jennie playfully tossed the apple to Ethan.

Ethan barely glanced up as he snatched the apple out of the air. Jennie was astonished by his lightning-fast reflexes. Ethan smiled at her and took a bite of the apple. The muscles in his strong jaw flexed as he chewed. Jennie sat down next to him to eat her own apple. She watched his bicep bulge under the sleeve of his tunic as he brought the apple up to his mouth for another bite. She secretly wondered what it would feel like to have those arms wrapped around her. The thought gave her delighted chills.

"Thanks for the apple. How was your outing?" Ethan asked her.

"Surprisingly informative, but I'll wait for Belle and Travis to get back before I get into that. They need to hear it too. In the meantime, I want to know more about you."

"All right," Ethan said. "What do you want to know?"

"Well…" Jennie's mind went blank and she couldn't remember what she wanted to ask him. Before she could think of anything of importance, she blurted out "What's your favorite color?" She made a funny face at how ridiculous that question was.

Ethan laughed. "Blue. Like your eyes."

Jennie's cheeks turned hot. He noticed her eye color. She felt like the apple she had just eaten was dancing in her stomach. "Sorry, that was a silly question."

"If you never asked, how would you ever know?" Ethan fixed his playful green eyes on hers. He started listing things off on his fingers. "I am eighteen years old, my favorite food is fish, my favorite hobby is climbing trees, I'm skilled with a knife and bow, and I have a newfound love of horses."

Jennie smiled. "What's it like living outside of the wall?"

"You always have to be on guard, and you live in constant danger of encountering lemerons. However, despite all of the dangers, it's wonderful. There is freedom like you have probably never experienced. You can wander as far as you like and the forest always guides you, revealing new and amazing things. My people and I don't live in a town such as this. Instead, we live within the trees themselves. We build our homes above the ground in the tree branches."

Ethan looked wistful as he continued. "Sometimes on a clear night, I like to climb as high as I can in the treetops and just sit there, gazing up at the stars. When I look up at the night sky and see how vast and beautiful it is, my troubles seem to fade away, at least for a little while. I know it must seem ridiculous."

"It's not ridiculous at all," she replied softly. "After what happened to my mother, I also sought comfort from above. I would often lie in the apple orchard peering at the sky between the branches and trace shapes in the stars. It sounds silly, but I helped me to think my mother was now one of the bright stars hanging peacefully in the sky far above."

A flood of emotion overcame Jennie, and she trembled.

Ethan came closer to Jennie and put his right arm around her shoulders. She let him pull her into a hug, and she instinctively buried her face into his shoulder. Breathing in his earthy aroma, she felt comforted. Maybe on those lonely nights both she and Ethan had gazed at the same stars, being far away from each other, yet connected in some way.

Ethan's hand gently touched her chin and lifted her face so that they were staring into each other's eyes. He kissed her gently on the lips. Electricity tingled through her entire body. She felt all her sorrows drift away. His lips were warm, like soft pillows touching her lips.

Jennie closed her eyes and kissed him back, wrapping her arms around Ethan's neck as she melted into him. She had never felt so happy, and she wanted this embrace to last forever. *Perhaps this is what love feels like*, she thought.

CHAPTER 32

As Ethan kissed Jennie, he felt the pull of attraction toward her growing stronger. His heart beat faster when she was near. The sound of her voice was sweeter than any birdsong. When she spoke, her lips entranced him. The impulse to kiss Jennie had overwhelmed Ethan. Something about her made him want to pull her close and embrace her. Maybe it was the way the corners of her mouth always turned up into a little grin when she saw him. It felt like a smile just for him.

He was relieved she returned his affection by kissing him back. He ran his fingers through her silky hair and relished the way she felt in his arms. During this moment, Ethan was able to forget completely about the lemerons, the oppressive wall that surrounded him, the strange disappearances, and the fact that his mother, who abandoned him as a baby, was probably in another building not too far away.

Ethan broke the kiss and held Jennie's face in his hands. Her smooth, creamy skin accentuated her blue eyes and made them seem all the more vibrant. Her pink lips were slightly parted. She was beautiful.

"I – I've never been kissed before," Jennie said in a breathless voice.

"I'm sorry," Ethan said. "I've never done anything like that. I didn't mean to offend you."

"No, don't apologize. It was nice." Jennie's cheeks turned a soft pink color. "Have you," she paused and looked a little embarrassed, "have you ever kissed anyone else?"

"Yes," Ethan replied. He saw her face fall. He added "my grandmother. I kissed her on the cheek before I left a few days back."

"Don't tease," she nudged him playfully.

"Sorry, I was only joking." Ethan said, "To answer your question, no. You are the first girl I have ever kissed. I'm glad it was you."

Jennie smiled and shifted so she was sitting side by side with him. She reached out to the makeshift table and picked up the paper with the graphite rubbing. "I saw you were studying this when I came in. Do you recognize the symbol at all?"

"It's the strangest thing," Ethan said. "I know I have seen this horse image before, but I can't recall where."

"This is a rubbing I made from the embossed image on the cover of Marlene's journal." Jennie said. "Maybe it has something to do with her?"

"It could be possible that my mother and the horse symbol are somehow related. After all, this instance of the symbol came directly from her journal. I know I have seen this symbol before. Multiple times, too, but I can't place where."

Something bothered Ethan about that symbol. He was searching his mind for an answer that would not come. Ethan closed his eyes tightly and searched the back of his eyelids for the memory. Every time he felt close to placing it, the recollection would elude him. It was like trying to grasp smoke with his bare hands. Sighing with disappointment, Ethan opened his eyes and shook his head.

"It will come to you," Jennie said.

They were both startled by a loud bang from below. There was a great commotion, and a horse whinnied loudly. Jennie's eyes widened, and she jumped up. "It's happening."

Ethan thought the worst. "What's happening? Have we been found out? Is this person Sash here to take us away?"

Jennie didn't answer. Instead she ran to the ladder and was preparing to go down below where the noise came from. Ethan stood up to follow her.

"Wait." Ethan called after her. "What's going on?"

Jennie's head disappeared through the opening in the loft floor as she descended the ladder. A few moments later, he found himself climbing down after her. The pain in his left arm was intense as the injured muscles strained during his rapid descent. This was the most he had used his upper body since the attack. He always took care when using his injured limb, but there was no time for caution now. Jennie could be in danger.

When he reached the ground, he realized that he had forgotten his knife on the crate. Silently he cursed himself. It was too late now; he would have to make do without it. The adrenaline coursing through him made his limbs feel lighter. Even if his opponent was stronger, he was certain he could be faster. He was stronger than most men and was a good fighter, but the searing pain would make his left arm useless in a struggle.

"Jennie?" There was no response. His eyes scanned the stables frantically, but she was out of sight.

CHAPTER 33

Anxiety crept over Ethan as he searched the stable for Jennie. He moved down the corridor peering into each of the stalls hoping to find Jennie or the source of the commotion. Coming from the front of the building were thuds and shuffling as if someone were in a struggle. As he approached the source of sound, Ethan could make out deep, heavy breathing.

Each stall he passed had its gate latched closed. He peered into each one through metal bars expecting to find Jennie and her assailant. Only horses were found within. One by one, he checked them all. Too much time had gone by. Jennie could be in terrible trouble and he wasn't there to protect her. He clenched his fists. He didn't know where she was and there were too many places to check.

By now, she might not be in the stables at all. Her attacker could have pulled her struggling from the building. He quickened his pace. The loose dirt of the stable floor muffled his footsteps. The gate to Misty's stall stood ajar. Ethan rushed to it and paused with his body pressed against the wall. Breathing heavily, he mustered his strength. He rounded the corner and entered through the opening.

The stall was empty except for Misty. She lay on her side, her swollen belly protruding high into the air. The heavy breathing was coming from the mare. Periodically, she would thrash her legs on the hay-covered floor, as if she were running. Everything about her looked normal except for something protruding from her backside.

Ethan stood transfixed, trying to comprehend what he was seeing when Jennie rushed past him carrying a bucket of water and her medical kit. It all made sense to Ethan in a flash. Misty was giving birth. The commotion they had heard from the loft was probably from Misty lying down and struggling to get into a comfortable position. Jennie must have known the situation, which is why she left the loft so quickly.

Ethan looked on as Jennie went to work helping the mare deliver her foal. If Jennie noticed Ethan standing there, she ignored him. She focused on was the task at hand. Jennie maneuvered so she was now near the rear of the mare to assess the situation. Jennie nodded to herself as she pulled on a pair of stretchy gloves.

The mass protruding from Misty was growing larger by the minute. Jennie carefully removed a membrane that covered the foal as it emerged. Ethan could make out its front legs and head. Misty gave a final heave and the foal slid free of her body. It had the same chestnut coat as Misty with a black mane and tail.

Misty gingerly got to her feet and turned to face her newborn. She lowered her head and smelled the foal at her feet. She began to lick its face and body. The foal reacted to its mother's contact and lifted its head. It tucked its slender legs in and with strained effort rolled from its side to its belly. Lying there, it breathed in the new surroundings through its small nostrils.

"Welcome to the world, little one. We will call you Buck," Jennie stood and began to clean up the area and her supplies.

Jennie returned to the stall, and for the first time since she left the loft, her eyes met Ethan's. She smiled broadly at him. "I bet you never saw anything like that before."

"No, not at all. I've seen birds hatching, but that was just incredible. You were incredible." Ethan took Jennie's hand in his. "For so long, I have only seen death at the hands of the lemerons. Watching a new life being born is refreshing. It gives me renewed hope that even though the world we live in is full of peril, good things are still possible."

Ethan still could not believe how calm Jennie had been. He was sure if their roles were reversed, he would have been petrified. She beamed at him. They both stood there watching Misty nuzzle her colt, happy to momentarily forget their troubles.

The door to the stable was slammed shut, blocking out the afternoon light. Startled, Ethan and Jennie turned around. Travis was bent over with his hands on his knees gasping for breath.

"Something's happened. It's Belle." Travis said between breaths. He swallowed hard and fear blazed in his eyes. "Sash took her."

CHAPTER 34

Jennie's blood ran cold at Travis' words.

"How did it happen?" Jennie asked, her shaky voice betraying her fear and grief for Belle. "How did you find out?"

"I saw it happen," Travis said in a small voice.

Jennie and Ethan were both silent as they waited for Travis to carry on. Ethan placed a hand on Jennie's shoulder. She felt both comforted and strengthened by his presence. She stepped away from Ethan, letting his hand slide off her shoulder. Pacing, she tried to push the fear from her mind to give way to more rational thinking. She had to keep a clear head if there was any chance of helping Belle.

"I got to leave early since today was my last day working in the kitchens. I decided to go to the solar farm to see Belle. I went to see if Belle had any luck getting more information about how Madam Marie was taken. She talking to someone, but I couldn't see who it was. I couldn't hear anything, but she looked scared."

Travis swallowed hard. "I wanted to see who she was afraid of, so I tried to get closer. That's when she started shaking her head and held her hands out in front of her like she wanted to keep away from this person. She backed up, and the person moved toward her. That's when I saw him. It was Sash. He was scaring her, and then…" Travis' voice broke off.

"Then what? What happened?" Jennie was desperate to know.

He took a moment to collect himself and continued in an unsteady voice. "Sash grabbed her throat with one hand.

He pulled a black bag out of his pocket with his other hand and pulled it over her head."

His voice caught in his throat, and he rubbed his eyes with the palms of his hands. "I heard her scream. I ran to help her, but I stopped running when I saw Sash take something else out of his pocket. He had a syringe in his hand and stabbed Belle in the arm with the needle. Her whole body went limp. I watched as he tossed her over his shoulder like she was a sack of potatoes and carried her away." Travis dropped to his knees in anguish. "I should have helped her."

"Sash would have done the same to you if you had approached him," Jennie hugged her little brother. He was trembling in her arms. "You did the right thing."

Jennie's mind spun as she tried to digest everything she had just heard. She played the scene in the classroom over and over again in her mind. Sash did not know their names or where they worked, and there was nothing that could lead Sash to them. Except for...

"Oh no," Jennie said, her voice barely a whisper. "The note."

"What note?" Ethan and Travis asked in unison.

"That's how Sash tracked down Belle. I'm sure of it."

It was the only explanation which made any sense to her. "Belle and I were the last ones to see Mrs. Townsend before Sash took her. He saw us when we were leaving her classroom. Belle had given Mrs. Townsend a note from her superior at the solar farm to excuse her from missing the first half of school due to work. Sash must have searched Mrs. Townsend's desk and found the note. It would have given Sash a link to Belle and led him right to her."

"Travis, what did you do after Sash carried Belle away?" Ethan asked.

Travis glanced sideways and stuffed his hands in his pockets. He wouldn't meet Jennie's eye. "I followed him."

"You what?" Jennie shrieked. She grabbed Travis by the shoulders and began shaking him. "Don't you know how dangerous that could be? Did he see you?"

Travis wriggled free from her tight grip. "I had to know where he was taking Belle. I was careful not to be spotted."

"How can you be so sure?" Jennie interrupted. "You shouldn't have done that. What if something happened to you?"

Ethan stepped forward and spoke for the first time. "Let him finish. He's the only lead we have to find Belle."

Jennie felt as though someone punched her in the stomach. How could Ethan side with her brother on this? She folded her arms and glared at Ethan. They just shared their first kiss together and experienced new life coming into this world. These things brought them closer, but now he was siding with her brother. She felt betrayed.

"Go on," Ethan prompted Travis.

"I followed Sash through town. He only walked down alleys. I guess he didn't want to be seen carrying a girl with a bag over her head. He wasn't far from the town square when he entered a small stone shed. I never noticed it before."

"Did you notice how long Sash was inside?" Ethan asked.

"I didn't stick around. I was the only person in the area and I didn't want to be there when he came back out," Travis replied. "After I found out where he took Belle, I ran here."

A daunting thought crept into Jennie's mind. "Travis, were you followed?"

"What?" Travis asked in a bewildered tone.

"Were you followed?" Jennie asked with more urgency.

"No," Travis answered tentatively. "At least I don't think so. Why?"

"We are no longer safe here," Jennie replied. "If Sash can track down Belle, it is only a matter of time before he comes after us."

"What do we do? Where will Ethan stay if it is not safe here?" Travis asked.

A plan formulated in Jennie's mind. "Today I spoke with Uncle Albert at the Apothecary shop. He knew of Mrs. Townsend's *and* Madam Marie's disappearances."

"But there hasn't even been a Commune announcement about Madam Marie, how could Uncle Albert have known?" Travis asked.

"There are other people in the Commune like us. Others who are trying to uncover what is really going on. They call themselves Truth Seekers. Uncle Albert is one of them, and he can be trusted. He told me that a secret group of people is behind these disappearances. Sash is only one of the people involved with our friends being taken."

Jennie spoke directly to Travis. "It is imperative you trust no one unless you are introduced by someone like Uncle Albert or myself. Unless you know and trust them, do not speak to anyone about Ethan or the disappearances." Travis nodded as Jennie continued to speak. "Uncle Albert has arranged for me to meet someone tonight that we can trust. The meeting will take place in the Apothecary shop. Travis, when I go to the meeting tonight, I want you to stay here with Ethan."

"Take me with you to the meeting. I can help." Travis protested.

"Travis, even though Uncle Albert is trustworthy, something could still go wrong tonight. If something happens to me and I don't return, let Father know everything that has been going on. I need you to do this." He nodded in agreement. Jennie turned to Ethan, "Ethan, please look after my brother if I don't come back."

"I will." Ethan took Jennie's hand and stared at her. "And I know you will come back."

A warm tingling radiated up her arm from where he held her hand. Jennie smiled at Ethan. She felt like she could breath a little easier.

Tonight she would meet with Uncle Albert and one of the Truth Seekers. Once she learned who could be relied upon, she would relocate Ethan to a safer place. Somewhere Sash would not be able to find him.

CHAPTER 35

Jennie felt like she would throw up. Sash abducted her best friend and she felt responsible. If she never took Belle to see Mrs. Townsend before class, Sash would have never seen them. They would have believed the lie that lemerons seized Mrs. Townsend outside of the wall. But then Sash would have found the incriminating book that Jennie now protected.

Was ignorance better than knowing the truth? The truth was dangerous. Belle was kidnapped because of what she knew. Jennie's lip trembled. She needed to cry, but she needed to do it alone. Seeking a moment of solitude, she left the stable and ventured into the apple orchard.

Mindlessly, Jennie let her feet guide her deeper and deeper through the trees. She cast out all of her thoughts and just focused on the gentle rise and fall of the terrain. The setting sun painted a beautiful canvas of oranges and reds in the sky above her. Jennie listened as a cool autumn breeze rustled the leaves in the trees around her creating a playful flutter of music. She inhaled the air that was perfumed with the scent of apples, although today it didn't smell as sweet.

On a nearby apple tree, a delicate leaf on the end of a branch danced in the breeze. Jennie stopped walking and watched as it waved back and forth, influenced by the unseen force of the wind. Jennie felt a lot like that leaf. Always being pushed or pulled one way or another by the confines of the society that she lived in. The more information that she uncovered, the more disillusioned she was with the Commune.

A subtle gust of wind blew through the trees, and Jennie watched as the dancing little leaf broke free from its branch and floated away. Her eyes followed as it was carried on the breeze until it flew out of sight. The leaf was free now, but Jennie was not. She began to cry.

CHAPTER 36

Sash rushed into Victor's study and sat across from him by the fire. His chest swelled with pride. He had tracked down a major problem and taken care of it. This was the kind of update Victor always enjoyed. Sash sat forward in his chair, eager to tell of his triumph.

"What news?" Victor asked.

Sash scooted even further to the edge of his seat. He found it hard to sit. He wanted to move about the room and pantomime the victorious encounter with the undesirable Belle. Instead, he gripped the arms of the chair. Since Victor was sitting, so too he must sit.

"I went back to the school and searched Eleanor's classroom. At first I didn't expect to find anything there. She's clever and wouldn't leave incriminating information lying about. I was going through her desk when I found a lead. It was a note excusing a student from class, and it was dated the day I took Eleanor."

Sash was speaking rapidly. It was hard to slow down. He was eager to get to the good part.

"It was all too easy to track down the curly haired girl named Belle Joiner at the solar farm. The note led me straight to her. If this stupid girl doesn't have what was stolen from the Secret Archives, I would bet anything she knows where it is.

"I wish you could have been there to see the panic in her eyes. She was terrified. It was so amusing to hear her try and deny any knowledge of the Secret Archives and what was stolen. The closer I got to her, the more she trembled. The best part was when I pulled out my trusty black sack."

He paused and looked at Victor, expecting him to beg Sash to go on. He imagined him saying to Sash, "Please, don't stop now. This is getting good," or even, "What happened next?" But Victor seemed disinterested in these details. He wasn't even looking up. Instead, he was examining his fingernails as if they were more interesting. Sash gnashed his teeth. He would not let this ruin him savoring the moment.

"When I pulled out the sack, her face turned white as one of your handkerchiefs. The girl's scream was drenched in fear when I bagged her. You should have heard it. She shrieked and tried to break free. I love when they struggle like that. To hear the fear erupt from their throats, it's beautiful. I tranquilized her and her whole body went limp. When the fight goes out of them, that's one of the best parts."

"So the girl denied all knowledge of the Secret Archive documents?" Victor asked flatly.

Sash was getting irritated with Victor's lack of enthusiasm for this great accomplishment. Within the past two days, Sash had procured three new people for processing. This act alone would accelerate the Order's plan by weeks.

"They all lie when they are first brought in," Sash replied with forced lightness, trying to hide his disdain for Victor. "Sooner or later, they all talk. I will find out where that girl's little friend is and I will get the stolen information. I have my ways of making people talk."

Sash observed Victor take a deep breath and exhale as he leaned back in his chair. Victor rested his elbows on the armrests and brought his hands to his chin, pressing his fingertips together creating a cage between his palms. Sash had been scolded in the past when he interrupted Victor's thoughts, so he sat silently for what seemed like hours, watching Victor think. The only sound came from the crackling fireplace.

Finally, Victor spoke. "You have not been able to obtain anything useful from the other two undesirables you brought in. What makes you think you will be successful with this one?"

"This one is young and weak," Sash shot back defensively. "She will talk. I'll make her beg to talk."

"You know I want no details of your intentions. What happens in the processing sector is entirely between you, Goggles, and the undesirables," Victor said, still with his hands pressed to his chin. "What I care about are results. I care about information and recovering that which was stolen from the Secret Archives." Victor lowered his hands and leaned forward, staring directly at Sash with the fire reflected in his eyes. "Do you know why it is called the Secret Archives, Sash?"

Sash slumped back in his chair.

"I didn't think so," Victor said with a superior smile. Sash hated that smile. "The Secret Archives are so named because the information contained within is dangerous and must be kept secret. The structure of our society is a very fragile thing. If this information gets out, then we will have complete chaos on our hands." Victor gestured towards the window. "Those people out there, those undesirables, they believe what we tell them. We tell them just enough to keep them complacent. This, you see, is to our advantage. If people were to learn from the documents stored in the Secret Archives, they would realize their entire way of life is a fabrication."

He softened his voice and leaned forward in his chair. "There are small pockets of people mobilizing to uncover the complete and unaltered truth. They call themselves the Truth Seekers. Should they unite and spread the information the Order so carefully protects, we will have an uprising.

We cannot afford for this to happen. Not when we are so close to fully executing our Grand Plan.

"The information Eleanor Townsend took from the Secret Archives must be recovered before the Truth Seekers obtain it. You have failed to gather any useful information from Eleanor or that cook. We cannot afford any more failures. The Order is growing uneasy. We have to produce solid results if we are to succeed in quelling this threat. You are a part of this Sash, and we need to focus on the bigger picture." Victor sat back and smiled at Sash. "I'm counting on you."

The contempt Sash felt towards Victor melted away. As always, Victor was only trying to protect Sash and the Order. Sash stood and puffed out his chest. He felt a renewed sense of determination.

"Soon, all of the undesirables and these Truth Seekers would be processed, and the Order will have complete control of the Commune. I will do my part and find out what Belle knows. That stupid girl will wish she had never been born." Sash placed his hand on his chest like a pledge. "I will not fail the Order again. I will not let you down."

CHAPTER 37

The wind was cold on Jennie's damp face. She sat under an apple tree and let herself cry. She cried for all of the things she couldn't change – her mother, Mrs. Townsend, Madame Marie. And she cried for the things she felt overwhelmed by – Belle's abduction, the Commune, Victor's deceitfulness. Despite all that weighed on her mind, Jennie felt better now after letting herself cry.

Jennie stood up and brushed the dry grass off of her pants. The air did a good job of drying her face, but the lingering salt from her tears felt like a heavy mask clinging to her skin. Jennie bent down and extracted her canteen of water. She unscrewed the top and poured some water in her cupped hand. Carefully gripping the canteen between her side and arm, she screwed the top back on and rubbed the water on her face with her hands.

She wiped the excess water away with the sleeve of her maroon sweater. Crying had helped. It was as though all her sorrows had drained away, releasing her from the burden of carrying them with her. She was still troubled by the recent events, but her head was clear now. The fog had lifted from her mind and she could focus on what needed to be done.

She bent down and picked up her bag, shaking off the dry grass as she did so. She slung the bag over her shoulder and replaced the canteen. Taking a deep breath, Jennie was prepared for what was to come. She was ready for her meeting with Uncle Albert.

Jennie looked around to get her bearings so she could head into town. During her walk out here, she had not realized how far she had traveled. She was very close to the wall and only a few rows of trees away from the end of the apple orchard. The strip of tall, unkempt grass that created a buffer between the wall and the cultivated land was within eyesight. Jennie walked toward the grass buffer.

Jennie had not returned to the wall since she witnessed her mother being taken four years ago. Tentatively, she walked through the thigh-high yellow grass. The soft seed plumes at the top of each shoot swayed in the breeze and tickled Jennie's fingertips. With an outstretched hand, she pressed her palm flat against one of the massive stones of the wall. It looked rough, but it was surprisingly smooth. Vertical grooves were etched in the stones from over a hundred years of rainwater eroding away small channels. The wall was scarred by time like Jennie; only her scars were not visible.

The wall towered high above her making Jennie wonder how her ancestors were able to build such a monumental structure which encircled the entire Commune. The forest beyond had taken her mother, but it had also given her Ethan. A mixture of emotions poured over her as she felt the cold stone that separated her from the outside world. Jennie used to think this separation was a good thing which offered her protection. The wall was no longer a symbol of safety to her; it was a symbol of oppression.

As she turned away to head back to town, a noise made her blood run cold. Not sure if she had imagined it, she stood transfixed, not daring to move a muscle for fear that any sound she made would drown out the noise if it came again. Listening intently, she waited. Just when she was ready to convince herself it was her imagination, she heard it again. Her hairs stood on end and nausea overwhelmed her. The sound was unmistakable this time; it was the low crackling groan of a lemeron.

Jennie pressed her ear to the wall in hopes that she might be able to hear the sound better. She couldn't be sure if it helped, but she definitely heard it again. This time the lemeron's groan seemed to come from a different direction.

She pressed her ear harder against the stone and closed her eyes, longing to know for certain how much distance was between herself and the lemeron. She heard a new noise which both surprised and frightened her. Something scratching.

Her eyes flew open, and she pushed herself away from the wall. Scratching. The lemeron had been scratching on the opposite side of the wall from her. In her whole life, Jennie had never known lemerons to come this close to the Commune. When her mother was taken, Jennie, Ethan, and her mother had followed the footpath about a mile into the forest where the best mushrooms were located. At the time, it was the nearest to the Commune a lemeron had ever been known to come.

Jennie pushed away from the wall and rushed backward. Her boot snagged on the wiry grass, and she fell to the ground with a thud. A sudden eruption of crackling groans poured over the high wall.

The raging groans and frantic scratching caused Jennie's hairs to stand on end and water to well in her eyes. The last time she heard a lemeron was when her mother had been taken. It was not possible for one lemeron or even two to generate a chorus of groans this loud. The harsh noise was coming from all around her. *How many lemerons are there on the other side of that wall?* she thought as the terror of what she had heard sank in.

Trying not to make any noise, Jennie slowly got up and backed away from the wall until the apple orchard again surrounded her. She ran as fast as she could to town. The horrifying scratching and crackling groans of what must have been hundreds of lemerons still lingered in her ears.

CHAPTER 38

The cold metal table was uncomfortable as Belle lay on her back, looking up at the blazing white lights through half-open eyelids. Everything was hazy. She saw movement above her which faded in and out of focus. She thought she could make out an arm, a gloved hand, and a strange face wearing goggles peering down at her. It felt like a dream. She was not sure if what she was seeing was even real.

Belle could not remember how she had gotten here. Where was she, anyway? The large white lights peered harshly down at her like adults scolding a child. A child. The word was familiar to her, and she remembered what it meant. She felt small like a child. Was she a child? Lying there staring into the white lights, she wondered what it meant to be a child or even an adult. Was she an adult, or somewhere in between? She wasn't sure. Was she even real?

Fingers. *What a strange word*, Belle thought. She remembered she had fingers, ten of them. They were a part of her, so she must be real. If she were real, then she could move her fingers. Belle closed her eyes and tried to manipulate the muscles in her fingers with her mind. Did they move? She couldn't tell. Maybe she didn't have any fingers, or hands, or a body at all. Maybe she was drifting away to some other dimension.

She opened her eyes again, wondering if the lights were still looking at her. They were still there, and they had friends. Two fuzzy heads now looked down at her, one with the goggles and another with narrow eyes. She thought she had seen the second one before, but it must have been a long time ago because she couldn't place where. The mouth of the second face opened and began making shapes, and she heard a funny sound. She didn't know what the sound was, but it was like some sort of muffled horn. She laughed and heard silly muffled noise coming from her. She giggled.

Belle must have made the second face angry, because it crinkled in an ugly way and its eyebrows came closer to the narrow eyes. When the face did this, she felt something bad in her head, and she felt her body twitch. Was this pain? Pain was a bad thing. Belle didn't want to feel any pain. She didn't want to make the face angry. It got angry when she laughed, so she frowned.

She watched the mouth of the narrow-eyed face move again. The noise it made was louder this time, but she didn't know what the noise meant. She didn't laugh, but the same pain ran through her body with the accompanying muscle spasms. She was confused why she felt the pain again. Maybe the face didn't like frowning either.

Her eyelids felt heavy and began to close, making the lights shrink. The faces faded away, and she could only see the inside of her eyelids. Belle felt like sleeping. Yes, sleep is a good thing. Maybe sleeping will make the faces happy.

CHAPTER 39

"What happened?" Travis asked as Jennie burst through the stable door. "I thought you were going to meet Uncle Albert."

Jennie could only speak between hungry breaths of air. "I went to the orchard. To collect my thoughts, process all of what has happened. I ended up at the wall. There is serious trouble there." She swallowed hard and took a deep breath then continued. "Hundreds of lemerons, maybe more. They are just on the other side of the wall."

Travis' jaw fell open, and Jennie saw his face turn pale. Travis and Ethan had been tending to Misty and her colt, Buck. Jennie had regained control of her breaths and made her way over to where Travis and Ethan sat on the ground near Misty. She sat down next to them with her back against the wall, glad to be able to rest her tired legs.

"This changes everything." Ethan looked at Jennie and asked her directly. "Are you sure there was a large number of lemerons out there, and not just a few?"

An uncontrollable shudder came over Jennie as she recalled the blood-curdling groans of the lemerons. "I'm pretty sure. The sounds they made..." Jennie swallowed hard. "There were so many of them."

"This isn't good." Ethan stood up. He paced anxiously, and Misty stamped her foot in protest. "This will only get worse."

"Let's talk about it away from the horses, Misty is getting upset," Travis said, breaking his stunned silence.

"You're right," Jennie agreed. "Misty can sense our anxiety. Let's go up to the loft and discuss this further."

* * *

Within minutes, Jennie, Ethan, and Travis had situated themselves around the wooden box table in the loft. "Ethan, you know something about what is happening, don't you?" Jennie asked.

Ethan shook his head. "I have never seen anything like what you described before, but I have heard stories from my people. Lemerons have a pack instinct. They can sense others of their kind and are drawn to them. As a child, I heard tales about this happening in distant places. The larger the group, the stronger the pull becomes on other lemerons, thus making the group even larger. It's a vicious cycle."

"Why are they drawn to each other?" Travis asked.

"I can't say for certain, but my best guess is survival," Ethan said thoughtfully. "A pack of wolves has a better chance of surviving than a lone wolf. When they gather in a pack, lemerons can hunt more effectively and catch more prey."

"Something just doesn't make sense. The Commune has been here for over two hundred years, and in all that time the lemerons have never come this close to the walls. Why are they drawn to the Commune now?" Jennie paused. "Ethan?"

"Yes?"

"Can lemerons detect people at all?"

Ethan mulled over the question for a moment. Jennie wondered if he was recounting his own experience with the lemeron that attacked him in the forest before he came here. "No. At least not in the way they can each other. They can see, hear, smell, and even touch people if they are close enough, but that's the extent of it."

"So, if I understand you correctly, they are not drawn to people. They have no pull towards us, correct? They only experience this connection with other lemerons?" Jennie asked, putting it all together in her mind.

"To the best of my knowledge, that's correct. Lemerons are only drawn to each other," Ethan confirmed.

Jennie nodded. "What about the dociles? Are lemerons drawn to them too?"

CHAPTER 40

Belle awoke to a dim room and sat up, clutching her throbbing head in her hands. She tried to recall what had happened. She remembered seeing bright lights and feeling intense electric pain ripping through her. It felt like a dream, but the pain in her head and body confirmed it had been real.

Belle rubbed her temples trying to piece her memory together. There had been two faces there in the bright room, two men. The first man she saw had been wearing goggles; she did not recognize him. The second man had narrow, cold eyes. She knew those eyes. They belonged to Sash. Belle shuddered as she remembered how he had taken her.

Sash had tortured her. That was the pain she felt; it was electricity. She had felt the occasional small jolt while working on the solar farm, but she never felt anything as intense as the electricity in that bright room. Belle found it ironic how the power she worked to generate on the solar farm had been used to torture her. This man disgusted Belle.

She looked around at the small cell, trying to determine where she was. Nearly everything was made of concrete: the floor, the walls, the ceiling, even the bench she had been lying on. The only thing not made of concrete was the blue glass wall to her left. Faint light spilled through the glass, giving everything a strange blue aura.

"This can't be good," Belle thought aloud.

Wanting to get a better look at where she was, Belle stood causing every muscle in her body to ache. As she made her way over to the blue glass, the constant throbbing in her head was equaled with the pain she felt in her limbs and torso. It had only been a distance of about five feet, but the effort of walking exhausted her, and she stumbled.

She put her hand out to brace herself against the blue glass and leaned on it for support. It felt warm against her palm. In the past, when she had come across this material, a docile was always on the other side doing the menial task assigned to it. Why was she in a docile enclosure?

Peering through the transparent wall of her cell, Belle saw what looked like a wide hallway which stretched as far as she could see in either direction. Lining either side of the corridor were enclosures like hers. She tried to count them but quickly gave up. There were just too many of them, possibly hundreds.

Panic set in as she realized this docile enclosure was her prison. Her hands began to tremble, and Belle felt her lower lip quiver. She had to get out of this place. Belle flung herself at the unbreakable glass and pounded on it with clenched fists. A harsh scream escaped her throat as the muted thud of her fists taunted her futile efforts. When her hands and arms ached unbearably, Belle sank to the floor with uncontrollable sobs.

Not even a full-grown man with all of his strength could break this blue glass. There was no way that Belle's small fists could do any damage. Belle surrendered to her dire situation, and her sobs softened.

Her eyes stung from crying and tears distorted her vision. She pulled the neckline of her sweater up over her face and used the fabric to dry her eyes and face. She sat there for a moment with her face hidden and her hands pressing her sweater to her eyes to soak up any fresh tears. When she pulled her sweater back down, Belle let out a horrified shriek.

A figure with yellow eyes stood against the glass in the enclosure just across from Belle. She didn't notice it before; it must have been concealed in the shadows at the back of its enclosure. This figure didn't look as gaunt as the other dociles she had seen. The skin was grey, yes, but its body still had meaty flesh on the bones, unlike the typical emaciated appearance of the dociles. Belle was puzzled by the peculiar appearance of this docile. Something about it was familiar.

Belle squinted her eyes trying to get a better look. She studied the docile for some time. It had a shapely feminine figure, and wore a blue dress. Belle wondered where she had seen that dress before. She gasped stale air and clapped her hand over her mouth in shock when she realized who she was starting at.

Removing her hand from her mouth, Belle asked hesitantly, "Mrs. Townsend? Is that you?"

The figure remained still, and the neutral expression remained unchanged. Belle was not certain if she could even be heard through the dense blue glass. The yellow eyes stared at Belle, making her feel uneasy. Slowly, the figure's head began to nod up and down.

With great pain, Belle pulled herself up on her knees and pressed her hands against the glass to get as close as possible. "Mrs. Townsend," Belle said in disbelief, "what have they done to you?"

Mrs. Townsend pointed at Belle with a slow, deliberate gesture and brought her extended index finger to her greenish lips.

Belle nodded. "I won't tell them anything, Mrs. Townsend."

With that, the decaying form of Mrs. Townsend turned around and disappeared into the darkness of her enclosure. Belle stood upright and banged on the blue glass with clenched fists. She had to get Mrs. Townsend to come back. She had to understand what was happening to her teacher.

"Wait," Belle shouted. "Come back. You have to come back. What are they doing to you? I have to know."

There was movement from the cells that neighbored Mrs. Townsend's. Before long, dozens of yellow eyes were fixed on her. Every blue glass enclosure that Belle could see, except Mrs. Townsend's, contained a pair of yellow eyes. The grey skeletal bodies of dociles were visible in the faint light as they moved forward, struggling to use their stiffened limbs. Matted, brittle hair clung to their grey scalps. In either direction as far as Belle could see, grey faces with gleaming yellow eyes were fixed on her.

Belle backed away, wedging herself into the rear corner of her cell. If only she could become liquid and escape through the pores of the concrete that pressed against her back.

Belle had never seen so many dociles before, and a nauseating thought occurred to her. Only a few days ago, Mrs. Townsend was alive and well. Now, she appeared to be undergoing some sort of transformation. Belle was deeply shaken by the thought that Sash and the man in the goggles could be turning people into dociles. She wondered if this same fate was in store for her. Tears slid down her cheeks.

CHAPTER 41

Night had fallen. Thick clouds blocked out the moon. Steady wind pushed the clouds, creating an ever-changing tapestry overhead of dark patches with silver edges. Periodically, the hiding moon peeked out through small breaks in the clouds, and intense beams of silver light poured over the ground before the wind slid another cloud in front of the moon, throwing the night again into darkness.

Jennie shivered as foreboding surged through her body. The wind carried a foul aroma, making her feel like vomiting. Hardly able to see in the dark, she walked along an alley lined with brick buildings. Her feet knew the way as she had taken this path countless times. Her fingertips gently touched the coarse bricks as she walked. She could feel a change in the air and knew she was approaching the town square.

She stopped in the shadow of the building and looked up into the sky. The wind carried away the massive cloud which had cast her in darkness. Moonlight shone down into the square making it look serene and peaceful. The water cascaded like liquid silver from the horse's mouths into the shimmering pool below. The area was deserted. Everything was still and quiet save for the fountain splashing. Even though Jennie could not see anyone, she still could be spotted if she crossed the square in the moonlight.

Jennie waited until a large cloud moved into place over the moon, blocking out the brilliant light. She sprinted across the square to Uncle Albert's apothecary shop. The display of bottles and distillations in the storefront windows stood like shadowy sentries, only watching as Jennie rushed past and entered the side alley.

An uneven cobblestone tripped her, causing her to careen into the recessed alcove on the side of the shop. Unable to slow down in time, she crashed into the door. Hot pain shot through her shoulder with the impact. Worried that someone heard the noise, she held her breath and waited. The night was silent. She was safe, for now.

Trying to erase the pain, she rubbed her shoulder. It was all she could do to try and clam her nerves. It might have been her mind playing tricks on her in the dark, but she thought she saw the symbol of the rearing horse branded into the wooden doorframe. As instructed, Jennie rapped gently on the door three times. It opened a crack, but no further.

Jennie spoke the password Uncle Albert had told her, "truth will find us all," and she was permitting entrance. She crossed the threshold, and the door shut and locked behind her. The familiar fragrance of ginger root, lavender, sage, and other herbs was stronger in this part of the shop. Jennie assumed the side entrance must lead to Uncle Albert's storage room.

In the dark, Jennie heard shuffling footsteps pass her. A door opened in front of her, and dim candlelight spilled into the small area where she stood. In the light, Jennie could see a small narrow hallway with old dingy coats and aprons hanging from hooks that lined wood-paneled walls. Uncle Albert smiled warmly at her while he waited for her to enter the larger room.

"Come, my dear Jennie," Uncle Albert said softly. "Our guest awaits."

Jennie walked through the door into the room which lay beyond. Uncle Albert followed her into the room and closed the door behind them both, sealing them into the windowless storage room.

Rows of towering shelves lined the perimeter of the room. An old ladder was precariously balanced against one of them. Arranged neatly on each wooden plank were beautiful glass jars and bottles. They contained an assortment of herbs, strange looking roots, and tinctures. Each bottle had yellowed slips of paper boasting the names of the remedies Uncle Albert stored here.

In the middle of the room was a huge wooden table overflowing with piles of scrolls, books, and blank sheets of vellum. A massive iron candelabra filled with lit candles was placed in the center of the vast surface. Positioned in front of a threadbare cushioned chair at the head of the table were an inkwell, feather pen, and vellum.

Scrolls and books were stacked in leaning piles on the floor all around the room. It was a maze to navigate, but the old man did it with little effort. Jennie moved forward into the room, careful to not knock anything over.

She found a worn wooden chair at the side of the table and took a seat. Anticipation gnawed at her. She was trying to imagine who the Truth Seeker she was about to meet could be. It might be anyone in the town, someone she only saw in passing or even someone she had known for years, like Uncle Albert. While she pondered, Jennie stared meditatively at the hot wax as it dripped down the side of the candle, slowly cooling on its decent. Each small drop of wax combined with those that went before, creating a mass that would soon be so heavy it would break free from the candle.

"Now that you are here, Jennie, I would like for you to meet someone." Uncle Albert sat down on the threadbare chair. "Actually, I am sure you have met her at one time or another, but not in this capacity."

Her. So, it was a woman. Jennie wondered if it was a classmate; could it be someone she sat next to for years? When did this woman realize the truth of the Commune? Was it thrust upon her as it had been thrust upon Jennie? She was eager to find out who this woman was. Even though Uncle Albert did not pause while speaking, Jennie implored him with her eyes to speak faster.

Uncle Albert went on, "She has been involved heavily in our movement. Without her, we would not have our connected network of Truth Seekers united under one name, one cause. We would still be just isolated groups of people working alone and talking in shadowy rooms like this one." Uncle Albert made a gesture with his arms to the large, windowless room. "She brought us together, and she inspires us to continue growing our numbers of trusted people so we can enact change."

"Albert, you give me too much credit," someone said behind Jennie.

Jennie turned. A tall, beautiful woman emerged from the shadows and crossed the room to sit in the wooden chair across from her. Jennie found herself looking into a pair of stunning green eyes. She knew those eyes. Those eyes belonged to Ethan. And Elder Marlene.

"Hello, Miss Caraway," Marlene said, "Welcome to our cause."

CHAPTER 42

Jennie had seen Marlene Saunders many times, but she struggled to recall ever hearing her speak. Marlene's voice rang out crisp and clear, reminding Jennie of the brass school bell's toll. Jennie had never been this close to her or Elder Victor before. She studied Marlene's skin for lines, wrinkles, or any sign of aging. There were none. Marlene wore the face of a youthful woman, yet her eyes reflected the wisdom of many lifetimes.

Jennie shifted in her chair. Victor was an Elder, and he was involved in terrible things. Marlene was also an Elder, but could she be that different from Victor? Jennie bit her lower lip as she tried to figure out how the two leaders of the Commune could be such opposites. Were they really opposites or were they working together and this was a trap?

"I understand your hesitation, Jennie," Marlene said. "You probably did not expect to find me here tonight. My position as an Elder allows me access to restricted information and those who wish to stop us do not suspect me. However, it also means I am doubted by new Truth Seekers I meet because of my proximity to those with questionable motives."

Jennie studied Marlene. "How can I trust you? During the Emergency Commune Council, you just sat there and listened to Victor's lies about Mrs. Townsend. She didn't wander off and leave the Commune. She was taken by Sash. I was the last person to see her before he took her off to who knows where."

Marlene looked at Jennie for a long while before she began to speak. Her tone was gentle and non-threatening. "You knew the truth. Why didn't you stand against Victor?"

"I..." Jennie stammered. "I had to protect what Mrs. Townsend entrusted me with. If I called out Victor's lie, who would stand with me?"

"You were afraid." Marlene stated it as a fact and not a question.

Jennie's cheeks flushed. "What could I do? It was more important that I keep what Mrs. Townsend gave to me secret. That's what they were after."

"And so you remained silent. You let Victor propagate his lies."

Jennie looked from Marlene to Uncle Albert. Both were starting at her, as if evaluating her. She didn't like being scrutinized in this manner. There was something almost accusatory in Marlene's words. As if it were Jennie's fault that Victor is able to continue to mislead the people.

Her response was louder than she meant it to be, but she had to make herself clear. "One person isn't enough to change anything. If I spoke up, I would be the next one to disappear. But you," Jennie pointed at Marlene, "you actually have the ability to change things. You're an Elder and Victor's equal. People would listen to you."

"I was just as angry when I heard Victor make that false announcement. Imagine what would have happened if I stood up to refute everything Victor said. What would the people have done if I told them Victor had instructed Sash to abduct Eleanor?"

"Chaos." Uncle Albert said. "There would have been complete chaos. Understand, Jennie, the difficulty in handling that situation. The Truth Seeker's numbers are growing, but there are still not enough of us to reach everyone in the Commune. There are still people who have no idea there is anything sinister going on. Those people would have panicked. The situation would have been uncontrollable for both Victor and us."

"I know Eleanor is your teacher and you care about her. She is a good person and is fortunate to have someone like you on her side," Marlene added.

For a moment Jennie believed Marlene was capable of motherly love. Something in her tone was soothing and comforting. It felt genuine. Jennie could not understand how the woman who sat before her today, who seemed to genuinely care, could be the same woman who abandoned her son as a baby in the forest seventeen years ago. Jennie would have to find the right time to confront Marlene about Ethan. For now, she had to focus on getting some answers.

"You speak of her in the present tense. Mrs. Townsend is - is dead, isn't she?"

Marlene glanced sideways at Uncle Albert who was shaking his head. Jennie watched with uncertainty, as the two seemed to be exchanging silent dialog with small gestures and looks. Marlene's eyes fell back on Jennie's. Those eyes pierced directly through her, reading her, finding her innermost secrets. She shifted in her chair again and tried to avoid Marlene's unwavering gaze.

"It is time you are made aware of everything happening here in the Commune," Marlene said in her smooth, musical voice.

CHAPTER 43

Sash walked through a dark side street toward the town square. No one dared to cross his path. He relished the informal curfew the people imposed upon themselves. Fear of the dark and fear of Sash kept the townspeople and those filthy undesirables indoors at night. The Order saw a difference between the two: the undesirables were trouble, and the rest were there to be controlled. To Sash, they were all the same.

The cold air ripped through his lungs as Sash inhaled deeply; how he enjoyed the night air, his one simple pleasure. Tonight something was different. The air smelled rank to him. He rationalized the odor was probably from him spending too much time in the processing sector.

Goggles probably reeked of the half-dead dociles he spent all of his time with. That wormy little man never left the processing sector in the bowels of the Commune. Sash wondered when Goggles had last seen the light of day or, as Sash preferred, the dark of night. The only thing that man ever saw was his blazing white lights and concrete dungeon. At least Goggles knew his place, unlike the undesirables.

Sash passed by the darkened apothecary shop as he emerged into the square. Everything was quiet. His eyes scanned the perimeter of the square, hoping to spot an undesirable or two. He had enjoyed breaking up the secret meeting between the man and the woman, Madam Marie, the other night. He could still feel the weight of the cold stone in his palm as he smashed it into the woman's skull. Sash wondered if the woman had survived the blow, but he was too proud to give Goggles the satisfaction of asking.

The man had gotten away, and he hoped the undesirable would be foolish enough to show up here again.

He was disappointed that the square was completely deserted. He crossed the square and trudged up the wide stone steps of the Sanctuary building. He threw open the pair of heavy wooden entrance doors and let them slam loudly shut behind him. The building was dark. Walking past the large Commune Council hall, he entered the cold stairwell. The hollow space echoed with his heavy footfall on the tile steps.

On the third-floor landing, Sash heard voices from further down the corridor. The meeting was about to begin. He strode down the wide hallway and slipped inside the interior meeting room. As usual, two small oil lamps sat in the middle of the empty table. The light cast tall shadows on the walls, giving the appearance of elongated fingers poised to grab the people settled around the room. Sash took his seat next to Victor's vacant chair at the head of the table.

It was odd that Victor wasn't here yet. He was always the first to arrive. Sash squinted around the table assessing the attendees. One of them must know something.

"As our Commune Elder and leader of the Order, Victor always stresses punctuality. It is in our interest that we commence with the meeting." Isaac Fenske stood, his gruff voice silencing the subdued discussions around the table.

Sash found Isaac's deliberate use of Victor's passion for punctuality against him insulting. In the near twenty years Sash had known Victor, he had never been late – not even once. *Something must have happened for Victor not to be here,* Sash thought. His jaw tightened in distaste. Order brother or not, Sash was not compelled to like this fool, Isaac.

Having silenced those in the room, Isaac sat down. "Brethren, we gather on this eve to forward our progress in the implementation of our grand plan. In recent months, we have successfully rid the Commune of a great number of undesirables."

Around the table, the others muttered their approval at the success – the success which Sash and Victor were responsible for, not Isaac.

"We have been able to disrupt the Truth Seekers' organizational structure, effectively severing their communication networks. Without their ability to join together, we are able to address the small independent cells with ease."

With every word Isaac spoke, Sash grew to detest him more. This fool boasted about Sash's work as if he had organized it all. Isaac had never lifted a finger to aid in the execution of the plans Victor formulated, and Sash carried out. Yet, he was claiming these victories as his own. He glowered at Isaac with his crooked nose.

The door to the meeting room flew open and slammed against the wall with a loud crack. Plaster dust crumbled to the floor from where the doorknob punctured a hole in the wall. Victor strode in standing tall. Fury twisted his face into a hateful scowl.

"My brothers, we have a traitor in our midst." Victor's voice boomed with anger. He pointed a finger at the opposite end of the table where Isaac sat.

Sash followed the invisible line from Victor's extended finger to Isaac's chair. Sash smiled, leapt from his seat with eager, clenched fists and rushed across the room to Isaac.

"Traitor." Sash cried out. He swung his fist and it connected with Isaac's throat.

Isaac gripped his throat and coughed as he toppled backwards onto the ground. Sash jumped on him, pinning him down. He hammered his angry fists into Isaac's face over and over again. Each time he made contact, increasing amounts of bright red liquid would pour out of Isaac's nose and mouth.

Except for the wet crunch of Sash's fist striking Isaac, the room was entirely silent as the Order members looked on with stunned dismay. Whether shocked by Isaac being a traitor or by Sash's actions, he didn't care. The Order never wanted to hear the details of how Sash accomplished his work, but tonight it was playing out right before their eyes.

Isaac passed out and his pathetic whimpering could no longer be heard. He stopped squirming in a feeble attempt to escape. Sash stood up and turned to face the Order seated around the table. All eyes were on him. He couldn't make out the expressions of the others in the shadows, but the oil lamp starkly illuminated Victor's face– he was smiling.

CHAPTER 44

Victor dismissed the Order with instructions to reconvene tomorrow night. No one objected. Victor looked into each of their eyes as the members filed out of the room. Some of his brothers met his eyes with approval, and some stared blankly through him, unsure of what had just happened. Giving them time to let tonight's incident sink in would further secure Victor's place of power. Everyone but Sash left the room. Sash bent down to pick up Isaac, intending to carry him away.

"Leave him," Victor said. "Come with me."

He left the meeting room and Sash obediently followed. Victor climbed the winding staircase to his quarters. In the study, he lowered himself into his favorite chair by the fireplace. Victor extracted a handkerchief from his robes and tossed it to Sash.

"Don't get blood on my things."

Sash grabbed the cloth out of the air and wiped the red from his hands as he sat in the chair across from Victor. The fireplace was fully alight and the wood crackled violently in the flames. The fire provided ample light of course, but in the warmer months the heat was brutal. Soon Victor would have his quarters powered with electricity and no one would dare oppose the privileges he allowed himself. Not unless they wanted to become a docile.

"You did well, Sash. I can always count on you to do your best."

"I was only too glad to wipe the smug look off Isaac's face." Sash smiled down at his reddened hands. "How did you discover he was a traitor?"

"I didn't," Victor said in a lighthearted voice, almost a laugh. "Isaac's loyalty to the Order was never in doubt. His thirst for power – my power – needed to be dealt with. So, I made an example out of him."

"You were late on purpose?" Sash asked.

"Yes," Victor stated. "I knew Isaac would not be able to resist seizing control of the meeting if I were late. As expected, he assumed my role as the Order leader in my absence. Our brotherhood has no room for people like him. We all have our purpose, and we cannot pursue the role of another member."

"Do you think the others will believe Isaac was a traitor?"

Victor laughed. "Of course, they will. They will believe Isaac was a traitor because I *said* he was a traitor. There are no lies between brothers in the Order."

"Unless they come from you." Sash smiled.

"You are very perceptive, Sash," Victor said. "I'm glad I can rely on your unwavering loyalty to me."

Victor rose from his seat and took the bloodied handkerchief from Sash. He tossed it into the fireplace. He stood with his back to Sash, watching as bright, hungry flames consumed the cloth until all that remained was ash. The intensity of the fire ebbed and returned to normal as the ash crumbled, and fell between the burning logs.

"Now," Victor said, his back still to Sash. "If you would be so kind as to deliver Isaac for processing."

CHAPTER 45

"What do you mean they're creating *more* dociles?" Jennie couldn't believe what she was hearing.

"Mrs. Townsend wasn't killed after Sash took her," Uncle Albert explained. "She was taken in for what they call processing. This is where they start the procedure to turn people into dociles."

None of it made any sense. Jennie always wondered how the first dociles came about, but she assumed they were some passive offshoot of the lemerons.

"Dociles don't bite people, so how could more of them possibly be made?" Jennie asked.

"Science. They create dociles by way of science. Many years ago, I —" –Marlene's voice broke, and sorrow flashed across her face. As soon as Jennie registered the emotion, it was gone, replaced by Marlene's cool demeanor. Marlene cleared her throat and continued.

"Many years ago, I discovered a shadow society operating within the Commune - they call themselves the Order. They are the ones responsible for all of these disappearances. I observed them for years from afar, always careful not to reveal my intentions to them. The ability to create dociles was lost for hundreds of years, but the Order rediscovered it, and perfected it."

Jennie paled and the nauseous feeling returned to her stomach. The more she learned the worse it got. The group of people who were after her and Belle had a name. It made them real.

Jennie wondered just how many people were in this Order and if she knew any of them. Had they watched her? Had they overheard her talking? Jennie shuddered with unease as she felt invisible eyes spying on her from the dark corners of the room. She tried to dismiss the feeling and focus. She knew the three of them were alone here. It was safe.

"Seventeen years ago, I uncovered their plan to remove all undesirables from conscious society. You see, that is how they refer to us: undesirables. We do not fit The Order's mold of what they consider useful – or obedient," Marlene added. "Our scientists are currently exploring ways to turn the dociles back into humans. The Order has taken this scientific research and distorted it to learn how to create more dociles. That is their plan for us: to turn us into obedient, mindless dociles who are under their control. When I found out The Order's intent, I vowed to do everything I could to stop them. To do so, I had to make great sacrifices to protect those I care about most," Marlene fell silent, and sadness filled her eyes.

Ethan. Jennie thought as a wave of understanding spread over her. Marlene didn't want to give Ethan up. She did it to protect him. She wanted to go to Ethan right now and tell him his mother didn't abandon him. Marlene only wanted to ensure that he was safe.

"One of the Commune scientists found out how the Order was defiling his research and he spoke out against it," Uncle Albert stated. "His protest triggered the chain of events which led you here."

"I don't know any scientists though," Jennie said.

"You know his wife," Marlene said. "The scientist's name is James Townsend. His wife is Eleanor Townsend, your teacher."

Jennie's mouth fell open. "I had no idea Mrs. Townsend's husband was a scientist. If he was taken too, that explains why she chose to teach the forbidden topics in class. She was rebelling against the Order, wasn't she? Just like you – like us."

"It would seem that way, yes," Uncle Albert said.

"Mrs. Townsend gave me this before she was taken away by Sash." Jennie reached into her bag and extracted the leather book with the faded gold horse emblem. "This is your journal, isn't it Marlene?"

Marlene's eyes widened. "You shouldn't have that," She stated in an alarmed voice. "It's dangerous."

"Why did Mrs. Townsend have it?" Jennie persisted. She had to know how she fit into this and how she can get Belle back.

"Is that from the Secret Archives?" Uncle Albert asked.

"Yes. That's where Mrs. Townsend got it," Jennie replied.

"Jennie, if you are found with that..." Uncle Albert said.

"Uncle Albert, Sash took Belle. He was looking for this." Jennie brandished the book.

Uncle Albert's face sank into a solemn expression. "Oh, my dear. I'm sorry to hear about Belle."

"Why are they interested in this book, Marlene?" Jennie asked.

"If they control the information, they wield the power," Marlene said plainly. "I trust you've read it?"

Jennie nodded.

"Then tell no one. Put it away and never speak of it again," Marlene instructed, giving Jennie a warning look.

"So, what you are telling me is you won't help me get Belle back? She was taken because Mrs. Townsend gave us this book. We owe it to Mrs. Townsend to save Belle. If we don't, then the Order will have succeeded in silencing us." Jennie heard her voice growing louder and shaking with frustration. "I can't let them turn her into a docile."

"We cannot afford to run a rescue mission every time one of us goes missing," Marlene shot back. "If we did, then even more of us would be taken. We would reveal our individual identities to the Order and they would hunt us down. Our only protection is our anonymity."

"My dear Jennie," Uncle Albert said. "over the years, our work has been slow and methodological, but we are making progress."

"Progress? What progress?" Jennie asked incredulously. "Within a week three people have gone missing, presumably taken by the Order. And have either of you been to the wall lately?" Jennie looked back and forth between Uncle Albert and Marlene with challenging eyes. Neither of them spoke.

"Well, you might want to. I would not call hundreds of lemerons gathering just outside the wall 'progress' if I were you."

Uncle Albert's mouth fell open and Marlene's eyes widened. Jennie gathered her things and left before they could say anything further. In the dark little hallway, Jennie felt all of her earlier hope and eagerness evaporate. Despite having received valuable information about the Order and their awful plan, Uncle Albert and Marlene would offer no help. The Truth Seekers were achieving just that: they were only seeking, not doing. Jennie had to take action. She had to do something.

As Jennie entered the dark side street, she had to stand still for a moment to let her eyes adjust to the moonless night. The clouds parted, illuminating the area in a silver glow. She was about to step out of the shallow recess when she saw a massive shadow slowly staggering along the passage in front of her. Petrified, she didn't move. She hardly dared to breathe. The figure stopped abruptly and turned toward where Jennie was standing.

To her horror, Jennie saw that the distorted figure was a man carrying a body over his shoulder. The pale face of the man shone brightly against the darkness. Jennie could see a menacing sneer spread across the pale, beady-eyed face. Jennie had to stifle a scream when she recognized Jacob Sash.

CHAPTER 46

The penetrating chill of the concrete bench seeped into Belle's muscles as she lay staring up at the ceiling. The coldness permeated her flesh and numbed her aching body. She closed her eyes and tried to focus on anything other than being a prisoner in this wretched place. She didn't know where she was or how long she'd been here. The passage of time was marked only by a steady drip of water echoing in the hallway outside of her concrete cell.

Belle imagined the water droplets freezing in the frigid atmosphere of this place. She pictured a slender icicle gradually forming, growing larger and stronger with each solidified drop. The dripping continued, destroying her fantasy. The water was not remaking itself into something strong. Instead, it was falling into nothingness.

Drip. Drip. Drip. The dripping became louder, and faster. Belle opened her eyes and listened to the change in the echo. Her brow furrowed in concentration as the sound grew closer. Water drops don't move. This was something else. Footsteps. Someone was coming.

Belle sat up with strained effort. She swung her legs out and put her feet on the floor. If Sash had come for her, she wanted to face him head-on. She would not give him the satisfaction of him finding her lying down.

Belle stared into the hallway, waiting for Sash to appear. A figure appeared in her peripheral vision. She turned her head to face Sash. To her surprise, she saw the man with the tinted goggles staring in at her. She didn't know if she should feel relieved it wasn't Sash, or if she should be just as worried about this man with the strange goggles.

The oversized round goggles hid his eyes exaggerating the man's narrow face. Bony hands stuck out from the sleeves of his crisp, white lab coat like the ones Belle had seen doctors wear. His short brown hair was unkempt and stuck out in every direction. What little pale skin was visible gave the impression he hadn't seen the sun in ages.

"I brought you food and water." The man pulled a foil packet and canteen from his oversized coat pocket. When Belle did not react to his offer, he stammered, "I – I thought you might be hungry or – or thirsty."

The constant churning of acid in Belle's empty stomach was a painful reminder that it had been quite some time since she'd eaten. For some reason, this strange man was thinking about her wellbeing. It was ironic since she recalled seeing his face during Sash's torture session with her. If this man was so concerned, then he should have done something to stop Sash from inflicting pain upon her. Perhaps he had though; Belle couldn't be sure. She didn't remember much of what happened, and her memories of the event were hazy.

Not wanting him to take her silence for refusal, and risk him walking away with her food and water, Belle said, "Yes, I am."

This seemed to please him. He smiled at her and opened a small pass-through window at the bottom of the blue glass. He slid the food and water through the opening before closing it. Belle hadn't noticed the outline of the window in the glass before. It looked just large enough to fit her hand through, but no more. Despite the small discovery of the opening, she didn't feel any better. It did nothing to help her escape from this oppressive concrete room.

Belle eyed him watching her as she approached her meal. Scooping up the foil packet and water, she made her way back to her bench and sat. It was uncomfortable to have him staring at her like this, watching her every move with anonymous eyes cloaked by the tint of his goggles. Hunger overwhelmed her. The neatly wrapped food emanated warmth in her hand. Turning her attention away from him, Belle ripped open the foil packet. She could have cried with delight as she examined the contents.

A buttery roll of bread, bright yellow corn-on-the-cob, green beans, and a fried lentil cake were all beautifully displayed before her. Belle eagerly ate with her hands, starting with the lentil cake. It felt amazing as it reached her stomach, warming her from within. She closed her eyes and let the pleasure of tasting the flavorful food overwhelm her.

"The lentil cakes are my favorite too," the man with the goggles said.

Without thinking, Belle's garbled reply came through a mouth full of food. "It's delicious." She realized her rude blunder too late and swallowed her mouthful. Even though she a prisoner, she could still retain her manners. "Sorry, It's delicious, thank you."

The man laughed. "No need to apologize. If anything, I should be apologizing to you. No one asks to be brought down here by Sash, and they certainly don't ask for what I do to them."

Belle lowered the bite she was about to eat. "And what do you do to them?" she asked, already able to guess.

"I give them a new purpose." He said, "I remake them."

That confirmed it. Whatever was happening to Mrs. Townsend was because of this man. He was responsible for her transformation into a docile. He seemed strangely proud of himself and of what he was doing. A chill ran down Belle's spine as she thought about the dozens of dociles she had seen in the neighboring enclosures. They were all people just like her once, and the man standing before her was the reason why they were no longer human. He did not strike her as someone who took pleasure in destroying people, like Sash. It was just the opposite. He appeared pleased with his ability to create, even if it was creating subdued monsters.

An idea formed in Belle's mind. This man created the dociles, if she befriend maybe he wouldn't want to turn her into one. He might even let her go if she executed her plan correctly. She forced herself to appear relaxed and continued to eat the food he had brought her.

"What can I call you?" Belle asked. "Do you have a name?"

"Everyone calls me 'Goggles' on account that I have to wear these," he said, pointing to the goggles covering his eyes.

"A fitting nickname," Belle said, "but do you have a *real* name?"

He brought his hand to his chin. For a long moment, he was silent, as if he were trying to remember. Belle suspected not many people ever visited him other than Sash, so it may have been a very long time since anyone used his actual name.

"Alex," he answered finally. "Alex Richardson."

Belle's mouth nearly fell open, and she had to fight hard to retain her composure. Alex Richardson was only a few years older than herself and had been a brilliant scientist in the Commune. He had excelled in his field, genetic research, so quickly he was soon the head of his science division at the young age of fifteen. In the technical divisions of the Commune, this was nearly unheard of.

The entire Commune knew who he was and followed his advancement with great interest. His superior abilities promised new scientific achievements for the Commune. That was, until he vanished under mysterious circumstances. No announcement was made, no Emergency Commune Council, nothing. He just disappeared. People came to their own conclusions about what happened and eventually stopped talking about him altogether. Some said he left the Commune to expand his knowledge; others said he had a terrible accident in his lab and perished, but no one knew for certain.

"Alex, it is nice to meet you. I'm Belle," she said with a forced smile.

"I like talking to you, Belle. You're a lot nicer than Sash."

"So are you," she said, not needing to force her smile this time. She could see that he was also amused and she decided to probe for information. "You mentioned earlier you have to wear those goggles. Why is that?"

"Before I came down here, I had an accident with my chemicals. My eyes were damaged, and they are extremely sensitive now. I have to wear them so the lights don't hurt my eyes," Alex said.

"That's terrible," Belle remarked. "Did the chemicals impact how well you can see?"

"My vision has suffered. I can't see as clearly as I once could, but the goggles help." Alex replied. "After the accident, bright lights and the sun hurt my eyes, so I moved my lab underground to this abandoned sector. I worked in the dark until I was able to fashion a pair of goggles which protected my eyes from the light. I grew so accustomed to it down here that I just stayed."

So that's *what really happened to Alex. He had an accident and went subterranean,* Belle thought. Sash must have found Alex down here and decided to use him. With Alex's brilliant scientific abilities, Sash would be able to use him exclusively for his nefarious purposes.

"Do you ever miss being above ground, Alex?" Belle asked.

Alex considered the question. "I enjoy my solitude down here. I'm free to keep to myself and work in my lab."

"I miss it," Belle said, answering her own question. She had to get him to see it from her point of view. "I miss the fresh air in my lungs and the feel of the breeze against my skin. I miss the beautiful colors of the flowers and the trees. And most of all, I miss the openness."

A silence hung in the air and Belle wondered if her tactic had backfired.

"The sky," Alex said at last. "I do miss the sky."

"Can you describe it to me?" Belle inquired. She wanted him to really remember the sky, to long for it. She wanted him to miss it so much he would let her go and they would both leave this forsaken place to look at the sky. At least, that would be the pretext.

"Describe it?" Alex asked frowning. "I'll try."

Belle closed her eyes to picture how Alex's version of the sky would look.

"The sky was blue everywhere, like a gigantic floating lake. I remember soft puffs of white floating along, changing shapes with the movement of the air. When the sun set, the white clouds took on brilliant hues of red, orange, and purple. At night, the blue water of the floating lake would vanish, exposing blackness with tiny points of suspended light."

Belle opened her eyes and saw that Alex was smiling at the memory. She smiled at him. "That was beautiful. We can go see it, if you like."

Alex's smile fell, and concern flooded his face. "I can't." He shook his head vigorously. "They wouldn't like it if I left. They really wouldn't like it if you left."

Belle didn't know who 'they' were, but she went along with it. "They might not mind if we only left for a moment or two." She had no intention of ever returning here if Alex let her out, but there was no need for him to know that.

"I'm sorry, I can't." Alex was still shaking his head. "I just wanted to see if you were hungry. I'd better be going now." He turned and scurried away with his head down.

"Alex," Belle called after him, but he didn't come back into view or say anything. Needing to stay on his good side, she added, "Thank you."

It may have been foolish to ask Alex to release her in their first one-on-one encounter, but she had to try. Belle would keep trying until she was free from this miserable place.

CHAPTER 47

Time stood still as Jennie huddled in the shallow recess. Sash was prowling the small side street in front of her with a man carelessly tossed over his shoulder. Jennie didn't dare to move for fear of ending up like the man Sash was carrying. Jennie's heartbeat thundered in her ears.

Closing her eyes, Jennie pretended that if she couldn't see Sash, he couldn't see her. Her mother used to play this game with Jennie as a child. "Where did you go?" Jennie's mother would exclaim when Jennie covered her eyes with her hands. "I can't see you, Jennie. You vanished." She remembered giggling and removing her hands from her eyes to look at her mother. "There you are," her mother would say, tickling her while they both laughed. In this present moment, she wished that by closing her eyes, she could become invisible.

She opened her eyes. Sash was still there, trudging forward with his latest victim weighing him down. To Jennie's relief, he traveled past the small niche where she was hiding. She counted to twenty in her mind, then inched her head forward and peered at Sash's retreating back. He was no longer recognizable from this distance, but was distinguishable only as a dark blob. He rounded a corner and disappeared.

Confident the path was clear, Jennie stepped into the empty street. Exhaling deeply, she tried to steady her nerves. A choice presented itself to Jennie as she stood in the street with a dense fog gathering in the air. If she went left, she could return to Ethan and Travis. But, if she went right, she could follow Sash.

Travis had seen where Sash took Belle, but there was a chance he wouldn't be able to find his way back at night. If she followed Sash now, there was no question about being able to find her friend. Time pressured her to choose; if she delayed, she might lose Sash. Making her decision, she turned right.

Jennie crept down the street and came to the corner where Sash had turned. Peering around the corner, she could see the dark mass of Sash and his victim turning down yet another side street. Treading as quietly as possible, Jennie walked down the street and stopped just shy of the corner where Sash turned. The thumping in her ears grew louder as her adrenaline rose.

Carefully glancing around the corner, Jennie watched as Sash made his way down the narrow alley. It sloped downward, and she lost sight of Sash in the mist that gathered in the streets. The wind subsided, and the fog grew thicker by the second.

Oh no, Jennie thought, *I can't lose him.* Foregoing caution, she rushed into the alley to get a visual on Sash. She reached the mist he had disappeared into. The thick, cold air brushed softly against Jennie's skin and felt heavy in her lungs. It made it impossible to see anything, and Jennie feared if she walked forward, she could bump right into Sash. Instead, she remained still and listened.

Closing her eyes, Jennie slowed her breaths and tried to focus on what she could hear. The steady pounding of her heart faded into the background. Silence surrounded her. The night was still and quiet, not even the crickets or the owls made a sound. A faint scraping could be heard a few paces ahead of her, like boots dragging across the stone-paved alley. It was Sash, and he was close.

The scraping diminished, and Jennie could visualize in her mind Sash continuing down the alley. A metallic, grating sound rippled through the air, breaking the relative quiet.

What was that? she thought. The sound was followed by creaking– hinges. *He must have been unlocking a door.* Jennie thought excitedly. *It sounds like he just swung a door open.* As she expected, she heard the creaking again followed by the bang of the door slamming shut.

Jennie sprinted forward through the blinding fog, feeling her way with her hands. The stone and brick walls of the buildings that lined the alley met her touch. As she continued, the feel of the wall on her left changed. The stones were no longer smooth, but rough and porous with large cracks. Adrenaline coursed through her veins as her palm brushed over rough wood. Jennie ran her hands over the surface and found it matched the shape of a door. This had to be the building Travis saw Sash enter with Belle.

Jennie pressed her ear to the door in an attempt to hear any sounds coming from within. Nothing. She stood back from the door and inhaled deeply. She exhaled and watched as her breath mixed with the dense white fog that surrounded her.

With a trembling hand, she found the rusty doorknob and turned it. The metallic grinding set her nerves on fire. *What if Sash heard that?* she thought, panic-stricken. It was too late now. If he heard it, he would track her down, even if she ran. Her hand still on the knob, she listened. After a few moments passed and all remained quiet, she pushed the door open. The creaking of the rusty hinges amplified Jennie's anxiety. She stepped over the threshold and let the door swing shut behind her, sealing her inside with Sash.

A cold voice cut through the darkness, making every one of Jennie's hairs stand on end. "Hello, little girl. Why have you been following me?"

CHAPTER 48

"I don't like it," Ethan said, pacing Jennie's cramped office. "She's been gone too long."

"Jennie is probably still meeting with Uncle Albert and his contact." Travis hoped that by saying the words aloud, he could make them true. Like Ethan, he was concerned for Jennie's safety. His older sister had always been stubborn – a little too stubborn according to their father. If Jennie set her mind on something, she would follow through no matter what.

Ethan stopped pacing. "What if the meeting was a trap?"

"The meeting with Uncle Albert?" Travis asked with a laugh. "We've known him all of our lives. He would never do anything to hurt Jennie."

Ethan began pacing again. "Something could have happened to her on her way back."

"Could you stop?" Travis asked. Ethan paused mid-stride and looked at him with surprise. "Look, I'm worried about her too, but you're making me nervous, and I can't think," Travis said, rubbing his temples.

"Sorry." Ethan took a seat across from Travis. "I just don't have a good feeling about this. Especially not after what Jennie told us about the lemerons gathering outside the wall."

Travis closed his eyes and sighed deeply. He opened them and held Ethan's stare. "I think Jennie may have gone after Belle."

Ethan's expression told Travis this was not what Ethan expected him to say. "Alone? But - she could be in serious danger. These people have been systematically taking out anyone who has been in contact with the documents Jennie is carrying. I can't believe she would just deliver herself right to them." Ethan paused and swallowed hard. "If they have Jennie, we might not ever see her again."

"So," Travis said. "What are we going to do about it?"

Ethan eyed Travis sideways, reading into the unspoken suggestion. "Let's go," he said, leaping to his feet.

CHAPTER 49

Ethan was encouraged to see Travis was becoming stronger in his own right. When he'd first met him, Ethan saw a haunted young boy tormented by fear. Travis had shown great courage lately by meeting his anxieties and challenges head on; he was growing into a man. Ethan could remember his own turning point when he took the step into manhood.

* * *

"Ethan, my boy, today I will teach you how to hunt," his father said.

Ethan was excited. He had just turned twelve and this was his chance to apply his skills as a ranger and a hunter. He'd spent his entire life acquiring these skills and now it was time to put them to the test. He and his father gathered their supplies and set out deep into the forest where the deer collected. After walking for what seemed hours, they finally came upon a ridge which overlooked the small valley below. A small group of deer emerged from the thick trees to drink from the stream flowing in the middle of the valley.

"This spot will do nicely," his father said quietly. "Now, take your position and ready your bow."

Ethan did as he was instructed. His father lay down flat on his stomach so the deer below wouldn't notice him. Ethan crouched down beside his father and took up his bow, pulling an arrow from the quiver on his back. The wooden bow felt solid and smooth in his hand. He gracefully raised the bow in his extended arm and positioned the arrow. With the blunt end of the arrow tight against the bowstring, he pulled back until the tension in the bowstring caused the wooden bow to arc back even further.

Ethan slowed his breathing as he took his aim. Just as his father taught him, he focused all of his senses on his target. Everything else which surrounded him faded away into nothingness. It was only him and the deer. The feathers of the arrow tickled his cheek as he peered down the shaft. He aimed at an eight-point buck.

His muscles were tense as he steadied the shot. Just as his fingers were about to free the arrow, he heard the cracking of twigs underfoot to his right near his father. With his bow and arrow still in hand, he swung his entire body to face the source of the noise. A lemeron was making its way to where his father lay. Ethan exhaled and released the bowstring.

His father pulled his gaze from the deer in the valley. He looked up in time to see the approaching lemeron crumple to the ground. As it collapsed, a terrible croaking came from the creature's mouth causing the deer to flee. The lemeron was dead. Ethan had slain it with only one arrow through the heart.

His father stood up and exclaimed, "Well done, my son. You didn't get a deer, but you got something better." His father examined the dead lemeron with his eyes. "I am impressed; you didn't even need time to aim. You are now a true ranger, a true hunter. A true man."

* * *

"Before we set out, we need to gather some weapons," Ethan said. "Have you ever used a blade, Travis?"

"No," Travis replied.

"No matter, I'm sure we can find something you can use for protection." Ethan looked around Jennie's office at the horse supplies. His eyes fell on the riding crop she had been brandishing when they first met. The small loop of leather on the end of the sturdy rod would certainly hurt if swung hard enough.

"This will have to do." Ethan handed Travis the riding crop. "I need to get some things from the loft. Wait here."

Ethan climbed the ladder and walked over to where his belongings were. He grabbed the small box of matches next to the oil lamp and picked up his belt, fastening it around his waist over his tunic. He secured his dagger in its sheath on the belt. Not knowing when he would return, he bid farewell to the cozy bed Jennie had made for him, and made his way back down to Travis.

"I'm set," Ethan said. "So, what's your plan?"

"First, we should check Uncle Albert's apothecary shop to see if Jennie's still there," Travis said. "If she's not, we'll need to retrace the path I saw Sash take when he was carrying Belle away. That's where she'll be if not still at the shop."

Ethan nodded in agreement. "All right, it sounds good. Lead the way."

CHAPTER 50

"Follow me and stay close," Travis said. They slipped out of the barn. It was still dark outside. Fog spread throughout the Commune, concentrating in the low dips in the land. The stagnant air begged for a breeze to come along and refresh it. A terrible stench greeted Travis' nose, causing him to choke and cough uncontrollably.

"Are you all right?" Ethan asked him.

"I'm fine. Thanks," Travis cleared his throat and asked, "What is that awful smell?"

Travis heard Ethan inhale. How Ethan didn't start coughing was beyond him. "That's the stench of lemerons," Ethan said. "I've smelled it before, but it's never been this potent. There really must be hundreds of them outside the wall."

Travis shuddered at the thought and hoped Ethan didn't notice his involuntary spasm. "Let's move on; maybe the air won't be so rank in the town."

Travis led the way, avoiding the main streets on their way to Uncle Albert's store. Before long, they had reached the edge of the square.

"There it is," Travis whispered. He pointed to a storefront a few buildings away. "The apothecary shop."

"I don't see any lights on inside," Ethan said.

"They must be in the back," Travis said. "Come on, let's get a closer look."

Travis and Ethan walked cautiously past the buildings which separated them from the shop. Travis stopped when they reached the storefront. The large windows had neat gold lettering which boasted "Apothecary Shop," and advertised some of Uncle Albert's more popular items.

They both peered into the glass window; Ethan cupping his hands around his eyes to see inside more clearly.

"I can't see much. It's too dark inside," Ethan said. "Wait. I can see a faint outline of a door. Yes, there is light coming through the crack at the edges."

"That's the door to the back room. This is good, Jennie might still be in there." Travis whispered hopefully.

"The light's gone out," Ethan pulled away from the glass. "Maybe they just finished the meeting."

They heard a door opening around the corner from them. Hushed voices drifted on the fog from the street which ran alongside the building. Travis strained to listen to what they were saying, but he couldn't make anything out.

He and Ethan crept to the edge of the shop and stopped at the corner. Travis crouched down, allowing Ethan to lean over him so both of them could listen.

"Foolish girl," came a woman's voice. "We cannot put our people at risk every time someone goes missing."

"She's upset." A man's voice, which Travis recognized as Uncle Albert's, spoke. "So many people around her recently have been taken by the Order."

The Order? Travis wondered.

"That may be, but we all have suffered great losses. She will get over it in time," the woman said.

Travis couldn't identify the woman by her voice. He was tempted to peek around the corner to catch a glimpse of her, but he was afraid of being spotted. Something about how she was talking about Jennie troubled him. Despite the cold, Travis felt beads of nervous sweat forming at his hairline.

"Do you think what she said about the lemerons at the wall has any truth to it?" Uncle Albert asked. "I have no reason to doubt her, but if she is right, this could threaten the entire Commune, not just our counterparts."

There was a moment's hesitation before the woman answered. "I don't know." A prolonged pause filled the air.

"I need to reflect on what this could mean. At first light, I'll investigate the wall myself. Get some sleep. I will be in touch."

With that, the door closed, and footsteps approached their position. Travis grabbed Ethan by his forearm. He hurried back the way they had come and pulled Ethan into a narrow gap between two buildings facing the square. Standing silently in the compact hiding place, they waited.

After a few minutes, a woman with long blonde hair came into view. She walked away from them, preventing Travis from seeing her face. Her stride was deliberate and confident as she crossed the square in front of them. Something was familiar about her. Just before she disappeared into the darkness, Travis realized this woman was wearing long robes. He couldn't distinguish the color in the faint moonlight, but they were unmistakably the robes of an Elder. "Elder Marlene," Travis whispered in astonishment.

"She hasn't changed at all," Ethan said through clenched teeth.

"What?" Travis asked, confused.

"She abandoned me as a baby, and now she's abandoning Jennie and Belle." Ethan's hushed reply was as sharp as his dagger.

"Are you saying…" Travis stammered. "Is Marlene your mother?"

"She's not a very good one, is she?" Ethan asked rhetorically. "Let's go find Jennie."

CHAPTER 51

Something slammed into Jennie's left cheek, and she let out a reflexive yelp. Pain shot through the bones in her face. Something wet trickled down her cheek. Jennie brought her hand up to her face and felt a sharp pain as her fingers found the split open skin. She lowered her hand and rubbed the viscous liquid between her fingers, astonished at how much blood there was.

Another fist found Jennie in the dark, and she bent over, clutching her stomach.

Not wanting to take another blow, Jennie knelt down and huddled on the floor. A frustrated grunt permeated the room as Sash swung again, this time with nothing there to stop his speeding fist. Jennie's relief was short lived as a heavy boot struck her side. Sash gripped her arms and pulled her to her feet.

"Trying to outsmart me, I see," Sash snarled at her. His breath smelled of spoiled milk. "That's enough fun and games."

Sash released one of her arms and tugged her downward. He was bending over to pick up something heavy. Jennie couldn't see, but she thought he was picking up that man she'd witnessed him carrying earlier. When he stood up again, Sash led Jennie forward, and she stumbled in the dark.

They did not walk far before Jennie took a step and found no ground beneath her foot. Her body was propelled forward by the pull of gravity and her heel caught the edge of something hard. Sash released her arm. Her momentum sent her tumbling headfirst. Jennie felt her body crashing against stone steps. She could feel blood vessels bursting in her arms and legs as each of her limbs slammed into the hard edges. It felt like being kicked by five horses at once. A flat surface welcomed her painfully at the bottom.

Jennie gasped for air as she lay on the cold stone floor. Panic overtook her as a suffocating sensation gripped her. With each distressed wheeze, she hungered for oxygen. She rolled flat on her back, desperately willing her lungs to work. An eternity passed before she finally regained her ability to breath normally.

Sash laughed as he knelt down beside her. "By the way," he said. "Watch out for the stairs."

Grabbing her arm again, Sash pulled her up. Echoing water could be heard as it dripped steadily from somewhere ahead. The damp, thick air smelled of moist earth. She was pretty sure they were underground now.

"Let's go," Sash snapped, and jerked her arm.

Legs wobbly from the fall, Jennie carefully put one foot in front of the other on the downward slope. Her body ached all over. Her knee was wet, like it was bleeding. Jennie wished she were anywhere but here and with anyone other than Sash. If only she had turned left when leaving the apothecary shop, she would be with Travis and Ethan by now.

Pushing regret from her mind, she strained to find an escape route. She couldn't make anything out in the dark. The air was stuffy, so she assumed they were in some sort of corridor. She didn't feel any drafts of air indicating there might be another passage connecting to the one they were in. So far, the only way out was back. It was unlikely she could break free of Sash's grip to run. She couldn't overpower him, so she would have to think of something else.

A light above a steel door appeared ahead as Sash pulled Jennie around a corner. From the faint glow, Jennie was able to determine they were in a tunnel. Water seeped through cracks in the ancient ceiling and splashed in puddles on the ground. Jennie wondered if the structure was strong enough to hold its own weight, let alone whatever was above them.

When they approached the door, Sash kicked it twice with his boot since both of his hands were occupied. Jennie heard scurrying from the other side of the door. A small window at eye level slid open, then closed so fast that Jennie was unable to glimpse who was inside. The door unlocked, and then swung inward.

Sash threw Jennie inside and her shoulder collided with the metal leg of a table. She gripped her shoulder to ease the pain. The brightness hurt her eyes, and she shielded them with her hand. After a few minutes, her eyes fully adjusted. The stark white room with metal furnishings only amplified the glaring effect of the lights.

"It's your lucky day, Goggles," Sash said to someone behind Jennie. "I've brought you two presents. One for processing and one for questioning."

CHAPTER 52

"Are you sure you know where you're going?" Ethan asked.

It was much harder to navigate the streets at night, and the fog was not helping. Travis searched the streets for the visual cues that would let him know he was on the right track. His heart sank as confusion started to take over.

"I'm sure," Travis replied, hoping the desperation he felt did not carry through in his shaky voice. "Everything looks different at night."

"So, you're not sure where you're going?"

"When I was following Sash earlier today, it was sunny out. And I was coming from another direction." Travis bit his lip and looked around. "This fog isn't helping."

His eyes darted frantically around, pleading with the darkness to yield and show him the way. That's when Travis saw it, the downward sloping street lined with red brick buildings.

"This is it," Travis said, in a hushed tone. "This way."

Fog enveloped them in an icy embrace as they descended the narrow pathway together. It was nearly impossible to see through he dense mist. He stopped abruptly, and Ethan bumped into him.

"Sorry," Ethan whispered. "I couldn't see you."

"I know," Travis replied in a whisper. "The fog is too thick. If anyone is waiting down there, we can't afford for both of us to get caught. We need a plan."

"What did you have in mind?" Ethan asked.

"We split up." Travis was trying to think what Jennie would do in this situation. The idea formed in his mind as he spoke. "The door to the shed is at the bottom of this slope. You wait here and I will go down first. If no one is there, I will whistle to let you know it is safe to meet me at the bottom."

"Let me go first, it could be dangerous," Ethan protested.

"Sorry, but you don't know where the door is," Travis replied. "It has to be me."

"What if someone *is* down there? What will you do then?"

Travis thought for a moment. "Then I will shout. Take that as the signal to get away from here. Seek out help from Marlene. She has to help you; she's your mother after all."

"No," Ethan hissed, "I can't go to her. If someone is down there, you shout, and I will come running to help you."

"But what if you get caught?" Travis asked, astonished at Ethan's stubbornness.

"I won't," Ethan said. "I've fought many monsters before. None of them technically human, but I know how to handle myself."

Travis saw Ethan holding something shiny in his hand. *His knife.* "All right," Travis said, "We'll do it your way."

"Don't worry," Ethan said. "If anything happens, I have you covered."

He had to remind himself Ethan had likely fought many times. Dozens probably, maybe even hundreds of times. Travis only knew of one fight Ethan had - with a lemeron. Ethan never did say if he killed the lemeron or not, only that he got away by climbing over the wall.

His stomach lurched with anxiety and he swallowed hard before speaking. "Okay, I'm going down there. Wait for my signal."

With unsteady footing, Travis crept into the dense fog. After a few steps, he turned to look at Ethan hoping to find encouragement in his eyes, but all he could see was the fog. He turned away and continued down the sloping street, keeping one hand on the wall as his guide. His palms were slippery with sweat, and he wiped his free hand on his pants. In his mind, he pictured Sash waiting for him at the bottom of the slope, wearing the same sneer he had when he took Belle. In his hand was a black, cloth sack ready to pull over Travis' head.

Travis tried to remain steady as he continued further down street and deeper into the fog. Pushing thoughts of Belle's abduction from his mind, Travis thought of Ethan and what he had said. *If anything happens, I have you covered*. Ethan was looking out for Travis. They were doing this together, and he was not alone. No matter what happened, their plan would work. It had to.

Travis wished Sash *was* waiting for him at the bottom. Travis pulled the riding crop from his pocket so he would be ready. He gripped the handle until he felt the dry skin on his knuckles pull tight. Unconsciously, Travis began running. He raised his hand, and he was ready to strike Sash with the small, fierce whip. The ground leveled out as he neared the bottom. Travis brought the riding crop down hard, ready for the snapping sound when it connected with Sash's body.

There was no snap. Only a vacant whoosh as the riding crop whipped the air. Travis spun around and swung wildly around him, ready to strike out at Sash hiding in the fog nearby. Whoosh. Whoosh. Whoosh. There was no one there. Travis was alone. Disappointment mixed with relief flooded through him and he let out a sigh.

He turned back around to face the door of the small shed where Sash had taken Belle. Travis nearly had to touch his nose to it to be able to see it through the fog. The door was so weatherworn it looked as grey as the stone wall it was set into. It no longer had the deep brown luster the other entrances in the Commune had. *This is it all right,* he thought.

Travis licked his lips and formed a tight O shape with his mouth. His whistle shattered the dull silence, and Travis waited. He heard the muted thudding sound from Ethan's boots as he came jogging down the inclined street. Within moments, Ethan was next to Travis with his knife drawn, ready for anything.

"Everything all right, Travis?"

"All clear. This is where I saw Sash take Belle." Travis gestured toward the door with his thumb, even though Ethan probably couldn't see the motion through the fog. "Knowing Jennie, she is probably already inside trying to find Belle. I don't know what we'll find when we get in there, though."

"There is only one way to find out." Ethan approached the entrance. Travis could hear Ethan's hands moving across the wood trying to feel for the doorknob. A terrible clatter of metal grinding against metal ripped through the silence of the night. Metal hinges screeched in protest as Ethan pushed it open.

"Do you think anyone heard that?" Travis asked, with concern.

"If they did, I don't want to wait around for them to investigate," Ethan said, "Come on."

Travis stepped past Ethan and entered the room. Ethan followed and the door closed behind them with another horrible wailing of hinges. Any hint of light was extinguished as the door shut with a hollow thud. In the darkness, Travis' other senses heightened to make up for lack of sight. His nose twitched with the thick, acrid smell of damp earth.

Travis said to Ethan, "I can't see a thing. Are you able to see?"

"Hang on," Ethan said.

Travis heard muffled fumbling followed by a scratching sound. A match hissed to life in Ethan's hand and radiated an orange glow. The little flame seemed as bright as the sun in the dark space. Travis looked around the room trying to find something they could use as a more permanent light source before the match burned out. Only stones laid into rough walls met his searching gaze.

"Look," Ethan said as he bent down to pick something up. He lifted a taper candle which was burned down to where only a few inches remained. Ethan touched the tip of the match to the wick. It lit without difficulty, and Ethan shook the match out before it burned his fingertips. The candle provided generous light and revealed the room they were standing in contained a single arched opening. They walked cautiously toward it and found a short flight of stone stairs leading to a passageway beneath them.

"Looks like we know which way to go," Travis said with false courage. He entered the archway first, and they descended into the darkness.

CHAPTER 53

Marlene entered her chambers to find the fireplace still blazing with light and warmth. She looked around the room, taking in her comfortable surroundings; the plush bed with soft pillows and thick blankets, the ornate rug, luxurious drapes, and expertly crafted furniture. This was indeed a place just over two hundred years ago she only dreamt of having, never imagining it could be a reality.

Back then, before they found the Commune, she had survived in the wild with her people. They slept on the cold hard ground with sticks and rocks mercilessly stabbing them. When she met Eric, they'd been fortunate enough to sleep in tents – unfortunately, that sparse comfort was short-lived, just like Eric. They were afforded no safety and had sleepless nights for fear of attacks.

Marlene sank into her soft chair by the fire and sighed. Perhaps she had become too comfortable here, too contented by the security the protective wall provided. The wall kept out the evil which lay beyond the Commune; however, it did nothing to protect the Commune from the wickedness that grew slowly within. She felt a pang of guilt for not doing more to protect the people from the Order. If Jennie was correct about the approaching hoard of lemerons, then Marlene had failed the Commune.

She rose from her chair and crossed the room to her wardrobe. She removed the box from the top shelf and carried it over to the fireplace. She sat down on the ornate rug in front of the fire, set the container in front of her, and opened it. When had she accumulated so many items? Marlene rummaged through her keepsakes, unable to find what she was looking for. She had to find it – she had to destroy it.

Her search became more desperate as she frantically dug through her possessions with both hands. Something sharp nicked Marlene's index finger, and she recoiled from the box. Her finger had been slit open, and blood trickled from the breach in her skin. Peering into the box, she saw her sickle. The curved blade that had saved her life so many times had turned against her to draw her own blood.

"Damn thing," Marlene muttered as she pulled the sickle from the box and tossed it on the chair behind her.

After blotting the blood away with a lace handkerchief she pulled from her robe pocket, Marlene resumed her search. She pulled items from the box and tossed them on the floor. Finally, she found the stack of pages bound together with string at the bottom of the box. The edges were smooth except on one side where she tore them from her journal. The accounts written here were too private and for her only.

Marlene held the brittle pages gingerly in her hand and looked at her faded handwriting. How foolish she'd been to write down her innermost thoughts and feelings. She couldn't bring herself to untie the string and read the narrative of her more recent past. It was too painful. She thought about the man she married in secret, about her son, Ethan, who she had to let go, and the evil taking root within the Commune. The pages held secrets she wanted no one to know – she could have done more for the Commune, but she hadn't. And these pages revealed too much about that.

Marlene tossed the bundle into the fireplace. The fire gratefully accepted her offering and flared as yellow flames licked at the edges of the vellum pages. The string instantly singed and glowed red with heat. It snapped, and the bundle came undone. The pages slid apart from each other and spread in the fire. Marlene glimpsed words and sentence fragments before the paper curled into ash, forever erasing her tangible thoughts.

Examining the piles of her possessions on the floor around her, Marlene found her old garments and gear from her days in the wild. She stripped off her Elder robe and threw the purple vestment onto the bed. She dressed herself in the tan, leather armor and pulled on her sturdy boots. Marlene picked up the sickle she had discarded earlier, and fastened it to her belt. The sickle was sharp as ever, her finger could attest to that. She didn't know how soon she would need to use it again, but it was best to keep it with her at all times now.

Marlene looked at herself in her mirror and saw a glimpse of the woman she had been. She looked the same on the outside, but inside she felt weak. Her eyes fell to the familiar rearing horse symbol that hung from the chain around her neck. It used to inspire her, now it overwhelmed her. It stood for something she was no longer sure she could live up to. All she could do was try.

Marlene pulled away from the mirror and moved back to the mess she made on the floor. She packed the remaining items into the box and put it back on the top shelf of her wardrobe. Returning to the fire, she picked up the poker and jabbed at the ashes. They gave way, crumbling into grey powder, leaving no trace of the papers.

CHAPTER 54

"Go and get the blonde girl," Sash ordered. "I want her to witness our little conversation with this one here. I believe they are old school friends."

Sash had ahold of the girl's auburn hair and was jerking her head around as he spoke. The girl winced, and instinctively reached up to protect her hair from being ripped out. Alex was glad he didn't have much hair; there was not enough for Sash to grab hold of, not that he would give Sash a reason to.

"What are you waiting for Goggles?" Sash demanded. "Get going."

Alex turned and went through the steel door leading to where he kept his subjects. Alex didn't care much for Sash or the way he treated people. Sash never showed any respect for Alex or the incredible work he was doing down here. He wondered what it would be like to have recognition for his work – being able to transform one living form into another was amazing to him. With each docile he created, Alex felt a swell of accomplishment.

Elder Victor had recruited him years ago, just after his accident. Victor told him of the incredible plans they had for the Commune. The plans would ensure the long-term resource sustainability and social structure stability for generations to come. Alex was honored the Elder considered him worthy to join the cause. Victor had given Alex this entire underground complex and anything that Alex needed. Victor even gave him research materials from other Commune scientists. Their research was studying how to reverse the docile condition. Naturally, Alex had to deconstruct it in order to extract the relevant components for his work in processing subjects.

Victor understood the amazing transformations Alex was achieving down here in his lab. Alex wished he would visit more often to see the endless rows of his successes. To Alex's disappointment, Victor never came to the underground complex anymore. Instead, he sent Sash to him with more subjects for processing.

Sash was insufferable. He did not care if the subjects he brought to Alex survived the processing or not. Alex hated failures. The subjects were more likely to fail if they were not in ideal physical condition. Too often, Sash would bring him injured subjects, some on the brink of death like Madam Marie. He shook his head at the thought of the wasted potential of these subjects.

The more he thought about it, the more he realized how much he disliked Sash. He always referred to Alex as 'Goggles' and never by his real name. In fact, no one ever used his real name – no one except Belle. She had been kind to him and even thanked him for the food and water he brought her. He had enjoyed talking with her. Since she worked at the solar farm, Belle understood science, and he was sure she would appreciate the intricacies of docile processing.

When it was her turn to undergo processing, perhaps she would participate willingly and not need sedation like the others. When she was a docile, he could still talk with her, but she would not be capable of talking to him. It seemed wasteful to lose a scientific mind like hers. Although, it wouldn't be the first time Alex had processed a fellow scientist.

"Hello, Belle," Alex said brightly when he reached her enclosure.

At first, she looked frustrated or maybe even angry, but when he spoke to her she looked at him and smiled. When was the last time he had seen someone smile? He couldn't remember if anyone had smiled at him before now. He liked that she was happy to see him. He liked that she was nice to him. Maybe they could be friends for the bit of time before it was her turn for processing.

"Hello, Alex," Belle said. He noticed that she looked at his hands, then at his pockets. "Do you have any more of those lentil cakes? They were delicious."

He frowned. He should have thought to bring her something. It was nice to bring things for friends, wasn't it? Alex made a mental note to remember to bring her something next time he saw her. He thought since he didn't bring anything he should apologize. That's what friends did. At least what he thought they did.

"I'm sorry." The words sounded right. "I will bring you some next time."

"That's all right." Belle was still smiling as she spoke.

Alex relaxed, knowing he had done the right thing. "I'm supposed to bring you with me. Sash has someone he wants you to see."

Belle stopped smiling, and she began fidgeting with her hands. "Who does Sash want me to see?"

"I don't know, but he said she is one of your school friends," Alex said.

Alex thought he heard Belle whisper, "Oh no," to herself. Looking at her more closely, he noticed her face was pale. Alex wanted her to keep smiling. He didn't like that what he said made her stop smiling. Maybe when she saw her friend she would smile again. Alex walked over to the numeric keypad to the left of Belle's enclosure and typed in a series of four numbers. The blue glass slid aside with a swooshing sound.

"Come. I will take you to your friend," Alex said.

Belle walked silently beside him as he escorted her down the hallway. Alex glanced sideways at her. She looked concerned, but soon Belle would see her school friend, and it would make her happy. Alex wanted to see his friend happy before it was her turn for processing.

CHAPTER 55

"I've found something." Travis called up to Ethan from the bottom of the stairs.

Ethan followed Travis down the stone steps, careful not to lose his footing. The candle flickered with Ethan's movement. He cupped his free hand in front of the flame to prevent it from going out. With each descending step, the air became increasingly damp, and smelled strongly of algae.

Ethan met Travis at the bottom and brought the candlelight closer. "What do you have?"

"It's Jennie's bag," Travis replied, holding a tan, cloth shoulder bag in front of him. "And Marlene's journal is still inside."

Ethan brought the candle closer to shine more light on the bag. There were stains on the fabric Ethan didn't recall seeing before. He pinched some of the darkened fabric between his fingers. It was damp. He brought his fingers closer to the candle and saw that they were red.

"Fresh blood," Ethan's stomach churned with worry. "Show me where you found the bag."

"It was right over there at the base of the steps, next to the wall," Travis pointed to the ground a few paces away.

Ethan stepped toward the area and knelt down. Reflecting the candlelight was a small pool of fresh blood near the base of the steps. Little red splatters surrounded the area and trailed up the steps in an inconsistent pattern that made him doubt Jennie had simply walked down the steps. Ethan clenched his fists so hard he snapped the candle in half. The top fell to the ground and was extinguished in a pool of blood. Ethan was left holding a stub of useless wax. A surge of anger flooded Ethan.

"We need to find Jennie now." Ethan said through gritted teeth.

"The candle's gone out. How will we see in the dark?" Travis asked.

"It doesn't matter. There's only one way she could have gone. When we reach wherever this tunnel leads, there is a strong chance we will encounter Sash." Ethan put his hand on Travis' shoulder to steady him. "If we do, you take this bag and run. Go to your Uncle Albert."

"Okay. I'm ready, let's go."

"Mind your footing in the dark," Ethan advised as he led the way into the tunnel.

Together they ventured deep into the bowels beneath the Commune. The sound of dripping water reverberated against the walls making the tunnel sound endless.

"There is a draft coming from somewhere," Ethan said.

"Maybe that means we're getting close," offered Travis.

They shuffled their feet to avoid tripping on the uneven ground or a root. A repugnant odor tainted the earthy smell of the tunnel. Ethan continued to feel a draft, but it brought no fresh aboveground air into the tunnel. After traveling some distance underground, Ethan noticed a distant light up ahead, slightly to his right.

"Look up ahead," Ethan said to Travis in a hushed tone. "It looks like a door."

CHAPTER 56

Belle was completely dispirited. Alex dashed all her hopes when he mentioned her female "school friend." He could only have been talking about Jennie. Sash had finally gotten her.

Belle's hands were clammy, and she felt a cold sweat breaking out over her body. She was unable to keep up her act with Alex, and she dared not look at him. Impressionable as he seemed, he was not on her side.

Oh, Jennie, Belle thought as a tear rolled down her cheek, *how did you end up in this terrible place?* Belle's mind was racing as she contemplated the scenarios. Sash could have found Jennie at the stable, or she could have been lured into a trap. A sickening sensation of guilt began churning violently in Belle's stomach. Jennie could have come searching for her.

Belle knew Jennie to be stubborn, but was she really so stubborn to risk her life for Belle? She closed her eyes to let remorseful tears stream down her face. She felt responsible for Jennie being down here now.

They reached a large steel door, and Belle felt Alex gazing at her. He cocked his head to the side like a confused dog. For all of his intelligence, he had very little understanding of human emotion. Belle resented him at this moment. If he could not understand the horrors of what he was doing down here, or why she was crying, then there was no hope for him. Belle dried her eyes with the ends of her sleeves and Alex tugged the heavy door open.

An explosion of bright white light hurt Belle's eyes when Alex escorted her into the room. She squinted and held up her hand to shield her eyes. The momentary strain subsided as her pupils contracted. Belle recognized the room; this had been where Sash tortured her. She hoped Jennie didn't have to endure the same. The sound of someone struggling drew her attention to one of the metal tables. That's when Belle saw her. Jennie was strapped down on a metal table, fighting against her restraints.

"Jennie," Belle cried out.

Jennie stopped struggling and looked at Belle with wide eyes. "Belle. Are you all right?"

"Never mind me, we have to get you out of here." Belle ran to her friend and frantically tried to undo the straps around Jennie's wrist.

"That's enough out of you," a harsh voice shouted.

A fist hit Belle's jaw, knocking her to the ground. She looked up at the towering figure of Sash sneering down at her. *Stupid, stupid,* she thought. How could she have forgotten Sash was going to be here?

"Goggles. Restrain this irritating little girl." Sash barked.

"Where am I to put her?" Alex asked. "Both of my tables are occupied."

"Tie her to the wall for all I care," Sash said. "Just keep her out of my way."

Both tables are occupied? Belle had hardly noticed the other table; she had been too fixated on Jennie. She slowly stood and backed away from Sash, up against the wall so she could see the entire room. On the other table lay a man who Belle didn't recognize. He was tall, with slender limbs and a bulging belly. He looked older than Sash by maybe ten or fifteen years. His entire swollen face was covered in blood, and his nose appeared to be broken.

Belle looked at Jennie, who had stopped struggling and was watching her. There was a large cut on Jennie's cheek and her lip was split and bleeding. Purple bruises were beginning to form under her pale skin. Guilt seized Belle as she thought of the terrible pain Jennie had to endure because of her. She had to do something, she just didn't know what.

Belle sidestepped around the room, always keeping Sash in front of her, until she was next to Alex. She spoke softly to him and tried to keep her voice steady. "I'm sorry I caused you trouble, Alex. Please don't tie me up, I won't do anything like that again."

Belle found Alex's expression hard to read because of his tinted goggles, but she noticed the corners of his lips turned upward ever so slightly. His faint smile seemed to convey a pleased expression.

"It's okay," Alex said, "You can stand over here out of the way."

Alex led Belle over to a work surface with cabinets beneath it. There was a window just above the countertop that opened into some sort of office with papers and diagrams covering the walls. Belle's eyes scanned the surface; it was littered with lab instruments, tools, labeled vials, and syringes. The syringes looked to be prefilled with different colors of liquids matching the liquids in the nearby bottles.

Belle casually leaned against the counter and slowly made her way closer to the colored fluids. When she was close enough to make out the words printed on the labels, she scanned them for something that might be useful. Stealing sideways glances, she read the descriptions for each colored liquid. Red was labeled "Phase III", orange was "Phase II", yellow was "Phase I", and the printing on the green tube said "Initial". These vials could contain anything. She needed something that would help her get past Sash.

"Jennie, I think it's time we play a little game," Sash said. "It's a game I like to call 'I ask the questions, and you answer.' The rules are simple. If you give me the information I need, nothing happens to you. If you don't answer, lie, or say something I don't like, you get shocked."

Jennie fought against the straps. "I'm not playing your stupid game," she shouted.

"That's what they all say…" Sash paused, then sneered, "…at first."

Sash moved over to a machine of some kind with wires on it and pulled it closer to Jennie. He took the ends of the wires and showed them to her.

"Do you know what these are?" Sash asked.

"No, and I don't care," Jennie spat out bitterly.

"Oh, but you will," Sash held up one of the wires. "An electrical current travels from this machine, through these wires, and finally to these round leads at the end of the wires. When the electricity reaches the end of the leads, it has nowhere else to go." Sash paused and looked into Jennie's wide eyes. "But don't worry. You see, when the leads get connected to something, in this case you, the electricity has somewhere to go. It will go through you."

Belle shuddered. It was all becoming clear now. She herself had been hooked up to this machine when she was here last. She could not let Jennie go through the same painful torture.

Glancing sideways at the countertop, Belle read the label on the next colored vial. Blue is "Sedative." *That's it,* Belle thought excitedly. She slid along the counter until she was closer to the pre-filled syringes. Casually, she rested her hand on the counter next to them. She looked out of the corner of her eye and located the blue one. There were four other syringes between her hand and the blue sedative.

Looking straight ahead, Belle watched as Sash finished applying the wire leads to Jennie's forehead with an adhesive gel. Sash flipped a switch on the machine, and the dials lit up. Belle's fingers slowly crawled toward the line of syringes. She counted as her fingers touched each of the glass tubes with a capped needle protruding from the end.

Syringe one. Sash asked Jennie a question.

Syringe two. Jennie spat in Sash's face.

Syringe three. Sash turned a dial on the machine.

Syringe four. Jennie screamed.

Syringe five. Belle grabbed the blue syringe filled with sedative.

CHAPTER 57

Travis and Ethan reached the door at the end of the tunnel. It was made of steel reinforced with horizontal beams. Ethan pointed out to Travis a small panel at eye level which could be slide open from within. The bare light bulb hanging above the door buzzed with electricity.

"How are we going to get in there?" Travis asked quietly.

"We need to maintain the element of surprise, but there is no way we can force this door open," Ethan whispered. They both thought for a moment in silence, then Ethan said, "I've got it. All we have to do is knock."

Travis raised an eyebrow at Ethan.

"Whoever is in there has to open this door for us and let us in, but we can't afford to be seen in case someone like Sash slides open that viewing slit." Ethan pointed to the panel recessed into the door. "What we need is the cover of darkness. We need to remove that light bulb."

"Brilliant," Travis agreed. "With the light out, Sash won't be able to see anything."

"Unless some light spills through the slit when he slides it open," Ethan said. "When that happens, we will be standing out of view on either side of the door."

"What if he doesn't open the door?" Travis asked.

"Then we'll just have to knock again until he does," Ethan replied. "Sooner or later he will come out to see who keeps knocking."

Travis thought about Ethan's idea. It wasn't perfect, but it was the best plan they had.

Ethan pulled a rag from his pocket and placed it over his hand to prevent him from getting burned on the hot light. Travis watched as Ethan stood on the tips of his toes and reached for the light bulb with his cloth-covered hand. Just as Ethan was about to unscrew the bulb, the light intensity wavered drastically from dim to incredibly bright. As the light fluctuated, a scream pierced through the air.

The scream sounded far away through the thick door, but it definitely came from a female. Ethan froze and looked at Travis. When the screaming stopped, the bulb emitted a steady, buzzing light again.

"What was that?" Travis whispered.

"I don't know, but that means its time to hurry. Get in position over there." Ethan said, and he unscrewed the bulb.

Darkness enveloped them, and Travis heard glass shattering as the bulb fell to the ground. Three deliberate knocks broke the silence as Ethan rapped on the door. They waited. The panel of metal covering the viewing slit slid open, and a small rectangle of light appeared on the ground between Travis and Ethan.

"What are you waiting for, Goggles? Let him in." Sash said.

"I can't see who it is; it is completely dark out there," came the voice of another man. "You probably blew out the light just now."

"It doesn't matter if you can't see him, you know Victor knocks three times. Do you want to anger him by making him wait in the dark?" Sash asked in a threatening tone.

Three knocks, Travis thought, *Ethan made a lucky guess*. The small rectangle of light on the ground disappeared as the metal panel slid back into place. Travis heard rusty gears grinding together as the door's locking mechanism disengaged. Travis swallowed the lump in his throat, gripped Jennie's bag tightly in one hand and the riding crop in the other. They had never discussed what they would do once they actually got inside the door.

The door swung inward, and Ethan's knife glinted in the stark light. The ranger lunged inside the room, throwing his elbow into the throat of the man who opened the door. He let out a croaking cry of pain and fell to his knees clutching his neck. He wore strange goggles over his eyes; this must be who Sash referred to as 'Goggles'. Travis tentatively followed Ethan inside with his whip at the ready. He saw Belle standing at the edge of the room with wide-eyed surprise.

"And just who might you be?" Sash snarled, as he crossed the room towards Ethan.

Sash was bigger than Ethan, and very quick. Meeting Ethan in the center of the room, Sash kicked at him. Ethan jumped left, but the heel of Sash's foot caught him in the thigh. Ethan grunted and stumbled backwards into a stand with a tray of metal instruments on it. The stand tipped over, and the contents of the tray clattered to the ground.

Sash took two long strides and was face-to-face with Ethan. Ethan hastily backed up and tripped on the overturned stand, causing him to fall to the floor. His dagger flew out of his hand and slid across the tile. Sash hurdled over the stand and approached Ethan, who scooted away from him. Ethan's left hand landed on a metal rod the size of a pencil with a small blade on the tip. He picked it up and jabbed it into Sash's leg. Sash let out a low growl and threw a punch. Releasing the instrument, Ethan rolled underneath the table where Jennie was, evading Sash's blow.

Sash growled with rage, and his entire face turned a deep reddish purple color. He reached down and grabbed the metal tool protruding from his leg. He ripped it out with a yell of rage. Sash dropped the bloodied instrument to the ground and lunged across Jennie to grab at Ethan, who had been working on unbuckling Jennie's straps. He leaned away from Sash and barely escaped his grasp. Sash's ears were turning red as the pigment of his fury spread beyond his face.

"You little blighter. Let's make this interesting," Sash snarled.

Sash reached over to the machine Jennie was connected to and turned a dial. The bright lights in the room flickered, and Jennie screamed in pain. Leaving the dial engaged, Sash stepped away from the machine with a sneer. Jennie continued to convulse. Each time Ethan tried to stop the machine, Sash lashed out at him, preventing him from getting to it.

Travis pulled the strap of Jennie's bag tight across his body and gripped the end of the riding crop hard. Running at Sash from behind, Travis raised the riding crop and swung at Sash with all of his strength. The stiff fold of leather cracked against the back of Sash's bald head. The pale patch of skin turned a violent shade of red. It had worked; Sash shook his head as if stunned.

"Go Ethan," Travis shouted.

Ethan rushed over to the machine and twisted the dial off. Jennie stopped screaming and lay still, breathing heavily with beads of sweat running down her face. Ethan snatched up his dagger from the floor and cut the wires.

Sash recovered quickly from the surprise attack. When he turned to face Travis, frenzy blazed in his eyes. Sash picked the boy up and threw him against the wall. Travis crumpled to the floor. Sash kicked him mercilessly and Travis curled into a ball, gripping his head in a feeble attempt to protect himself.

"You undesirables are all the same." Sash screamed. "You never know your place."

Sash released a furious scream. Travis curled as tight as he could to avoid the blow which was sure to come, but nothing happened. He lifted his head to see what was going on, just in time to see Belle slam a syringe into Sash's neck. Without hesitation, she used her thumb to push down on the plunger and blue liquid drained it into Sash's neck. She removed the needle and dropped the syringe on the ground, shattering it.

Sash brought his hand to his neck. He lunged toward Belle and reached out to seize her, but his eyelids drooped and he stumbled sideways. He tripped over Travis and fell into the metal table with the unconscious man on it. He tried to pull himself up using the table but his muscles became too weak. His eyes closed and the arm supporting his weight went limp. Sash fell to the ground unmoving.

"What did you inject him with? Is he dead?" Travis managed to ask Belle.

"No, he's not dead, he's only knocked out. I gave him with a sedative. I'm assuming it's the same stuff he used on me. I had been planning on sneaking up behind him before you came in. When I saw you two, I knew there would be trouble with Sash. While you were fighting, I was keeping watch for the right time to bring him down. I knew I'd only get one chance at it, so I had to be sure the timing was right."

Belle extended a hand to help Travis up. He shook his head and gripped his side. "Thanks, but I need minute to recover. I'm glad you knocked him out when you did."

Belle looked regretful, "I'm sorry I didn't have a chance to get to him sooner. Are you all right?"

"I'll be fine," Travis said.

He looked over to where Jennie was still lying on the table, breathing heavily with her eyes closed. Ethan was by her side carefully cutting the straps that bound her to the table. He walked to Jennie's head and removed the severed wires stuck to her forehead.

"Jennie?" Ethan blotted the sweat and blood from her face with a rag.

"Ethan? I am so glad to see you. What happened?" she asked in a scratchy voice.

"First we need to get you out of here, then we will fill you in on all the details." Ethan took her hand in his.

"Where are Belle and Travis? Are they safe?"

"Over here," Travis called out from the floor. Jennie turned her head looked relieved. Her body relaxed.

"Belle, do you know if there is any water around here?" Ethan asked.

"I think I saw some in the office." Belle rushed away.

Ethan helped Jennie to sit up, and she groaned.

Belle came back with something to drink, some packets of food. She opened the canteen and helped Jennie to drink. Water spilled down Jennie's chin as she drank, but the intake of fluids helped the color return to her face.

"Thanks," Jennie said.

"Take a moment to rest while I look around," Belle instructed.

Travis watched Belle rush back into the office. He could see her through the window dividing the two rooms. She was rummaging around and ripping papers off the walls. Stopping, she looked around the room with furrowed brow. Her face brightened. She rushed to the corner of the room and bent down out of view. When she stood back up, Travis saw her dumping the contents of a trash bin on the floor. She then began stuffing all the papers in the empty container.

Belle emerged from the office with the trashcan full of papers tucked under her arm.

"What are those papers, Belle?" Travis asked.

"I thought they might be useful. I think they are detailed records of what they have been doing down here. We can read them later and find out for sure."

"Good idea." Travis agreed. "Lets get out of this awful place."

Travis staggered to his feet. The effort just to stand was painful and draining. He clutched his sore ribs, panting.

"I couldn't agree more," Jennie said. "I think I'm okay to stand."

Ethan helped Jennie to her feet, and he looped her arm over around his neck to support her weight.

"Let's get out of here and rest. Then we can figure out what to do," Belle said. "No one will come for us as long as Sash remains unconscious."

"What about Goggles over there?" Travis asked, pointing to the man still sitting by the door to the tunnel.

"His name is Alex," Belle said. "And he's no threat to us right now."

"Let's go then," Jennie said. "I want to be anywhere but here."

Belle looked around. "I couldn't agree more."

Ethan led Jennie carefully across the room and into the tunnel. Travis, still clinging to Jennie's bag, followed behind them with Belle.

Belle stopped just before passing through the door. She turned to the man still slumped on the floor and said, "Goodbye, Alex. I hope someday you get to see the sky again."

Belle walked with Travis as they passed through the door and entered the tunnel. She didn't look back.

CHAPTER 58

Marlene did not sleep at all that night. She sat in her chair next to the window and watched the sky transform from black to a pale purple. The fire had burned out hours ago, and the chill of autumn crept into her bedroom. She was alone with her thoughts too often these days. Her mind frequently kept her awake and tormented her about the decisions she made in her past. The persistent thought keeping her awake tonight was the warning Jennie had given about the lemerons collecting at the wall.

Marlene stood and pulled her thick cloak on over her leather armor. The sun had not yet broken over the horizon, but the hint of dawn would give her enough light to see by. She glided down the tower stairs and out of the Sanctuary. Her stride was smooth, speedy, and deliberate as she crossed the town square and made her way to the north wall. The smell repulsed her as she crossed the apple orchard and grew closer to the wall.

An eerie silence hung in the air as she listened. When she reached the wall, she heard a low humming noise. It reminded her of the combined idle chatter before the Commune Council starts. Only this sound contained no words, no laughter, no voices in the traditional sense. In the past, she had heard the low growl of a lemeron as it traveled through the woods, unaware of her presence. What she was hearing was this same lemeron growl compounded hundreds of times.

Marlene was determined to see the source. She had to confirm how many lemerons there really were. Until she saw it for herself, she couldn't fully trust the assessment of a teenage girl who didn't actually see the lemerons. Marlene scaled the wall with ease. One advantage of her curse was that she had incredible strength. An average man would find this climb difficult, but to her, it was as easy as walking.

Marlene stood on the wide, flat stones that capped the thick wall. The rising sun brought with it a gusting wind that was amplified at this height above the trees. Marlene's hair and cloak whipped behind her in the wind as she stared out at the horizon. The trees had grown thicker since she had last visited the forest. She had not set eyes upon the woods since she brought Ethan out here for a better chance. Thinking of her little boy from long ago, her eyes dropped to the ground outside of the wall. Marlene was not easily unnerved, but what she saw made her shudder. A sea of slow moving, grey flesh concealed the ground. Jennie had been right.

Hundreds of lemerons were gathering at the wall. Marlene could see more approaching through the trees. Their deceptively strong limbs clawed feebly at whatever stood between them and the Commune. The closest lemerons scraped at the wall. Those that were further back scratched at the grey flesh of the lemerons in front of them, tearing their skin open spilling the congealed, brown ooze that long ago was blood. The lemerons were trying to rip through anything that stood in their way.

Marlene understood now where the stench was coming from. More lemerons were coming in from every direction. Alone, they smelled terrible, like rotting meat left in the sun for days. With a large number like this ripping at each other, the odor was unbearable. It had been many long decades since Marlene encountered the smell. She gagged uncontrollably and clutched her hand to her mouth to stifle the sound.

The lemerons heard her. All at once they stopped moving and looked up at her. Endless numbers of gleaming yellows eyes stared at her like a nightmare version of a star-filled sky. Angry mouths opened revealing blackened teeth, and an outbreak of simultaneous roars, croaks, and groans filled the dead air around her. The furious cries that enveloped Marlene were like a cage closing in around her, rooting her to the spot.

All Marlene could do was watch as the lemerons went into a frenzy. Their arms swung wildly, attacking anything within reach. She watched them rip at each other and slap the wall with open gnarled hands. They would not stop until they reached her or until she left their sight and they forgot about her. She would see to it that it was the latter.

Had Ethan ever come into contact with the lemerons, she wondered? Marlene hoped that he had been spared. Looking at the scene below, she could not be sure. The lemerons were vicious. They would spare no human, least of all a baby. Her lower lip trembled, as she thought of her innocent little infant; so pure, so perfect, and so defenseless.

She needed to know if Ethan's father had gotten to him in time. Marlene had to locate her son out there in the forest and enlist the help of his people. The situation before her had escalated beyond the ability of the Commune to manage. She needed to build an army. But before Marlene set off into the forest to seek aide, she had to do one last thing.

CHAPTER 59

Jennie awoke to the sound of the school bell tolling. She kept her eyes closed and begged for more sleep, but the bell continued to ring. Something was different about the chimes which carried across the Commune. The bell rang ceaselessly and it sounded almost – frantic.

Reluctantly, Jennie opened her eyes. At first disoriented as to where she was, Jennie looked around and took in the familiar surroundings of the loft in the stable. She was lying on a horse blanket spread over a bed of hay. Belle was fast asleep next to her, and both Ethan and Travis were asleep near her feet. Ethan clutched the handle of his sheathed dagger as he slept. Even in his sleep, he was still on guard after the events of the past few days.

Jennie sat up and winced in pain. She couldn't recall much of what happened when she was strapped to that terrible table, so the others had told her about everything. Jennie let them know about the meeting with Uncle Albert and Marlene. She told them everything except for what Marlene said about sacrificing Ethan for his own safety. That piece of information she wanted to share with Ethan privately.

Jennie peered down at Travis. He looked as battered as she felt. Despite all she had done to protect him through the years, he was the one who ended up saving her. Ethan boasted how Travis was the one who planned the rescue mission and how he had shown true bravery. Travis had become a courageous young man. She felt herself swelling with pride and her eyes watered.

Jennie knew that if it weren't for Ethan's help, none of them would have made it out of that terrible place. She crawled toward Ethan. The stubble on his cheeks had grown, and despite a few bruises, he was more handsome than ever. Sensing a presence near him, Ethan's emerald-green eyes shot open, and his hand gripped the dagger handle tighter. Jennie sat back on her heels and watched as awareness filled his face and his tension drained away.

"Good morning," Jennie said.

"Good morning." Ethan he sat up. "What's that sound?"

Jennie furrowed her brow. "It's the bell in the schoolhouse. It's been ringing constantly for a little while now. Something must be wrong."

"We should go check it out. It might have something to do with us," Ethan said.

"What if someone sees you?" Jennie asked. "People here believe there is no one left outside of the Commune. You disprove that, and they might not take it well."

"Let them take it however they like. There is no way I am letting you go without me, not after what happened last night. If Sash shows up, I want to be there." Ethan was unwavering.

"You're right," Jennie conceded. "It's time we held nothing back, including you. Let the people of the Commune see you."

Jennie took Ethan's hand in hers and leaned in to kiss him. The fluttering she always felt when she was near him intensified as she held the kiss. Even though the gentle pressure on her split lip hurt, she didn't want it to end. Ethan cupped the back of Jennie's head in his hand and ran his hand through her hair. The continuous tolling of the bell brought them back to reality and their uphill struggle against the Order.

Ethan broke the kiss and then gestured to Belle and Travis. "They're waking up."

Belle groaned as she sat up, and Travis rubbed his bleary eyes.

"What's going on?" Belle asked. "Why is the bell ringing?"

"Good morning you two," Jennie said. "The bell has been ringing non-stop since I woke up this morning. It's probably been ringing even before that. Something feels off about it."

"Do you think it has something to do with what happened last night?" Travis asked.

"I don't know," Jennie said. "But we need to find out what's going on. Be prepared for anything."

"If we run into Sash, we may not be able to come back here, so bring anything that you can't leave behind," Ethan added.

"Ethan is coming with us? What if someone sees him?" Travis asked.

"I really don't think it makes a difference now," Belle said scornfully. "I hope people *do* see Ethan. Maybe then they will start realizing all of the lies Victor and this Order have been feeding us."

"It's something we have to take a chance with," Jennie said, a little uncomfortably. She didn't want anything to happen to Ethan, and she wasn't sure wandering the streets was safe for him. "Get your things."

The four of them gathered their belongings and climbed down the loft ladder. Jennie felt saddened at the prospect of not being able to return to her horses. She pushed the notion from her mind and resolved to address the possibility if it should come up, and only then. They left the warmth of the stable behind, and Jennie slid the barn door shut behind them.

They walked together in a group through the narrow streets leading to the town square. As they got closer, more people emerged from buildings and alleys, joining the four of them as they walked. Jennie could overhear the uncertain conversations of the people around her as they walked closer to the source of the ominous tolling.

"What is happening?" one woman said to a stout man.

The man leaned in close to her as they walked and said in a hushed voice, "I heard we don't have enough food for winter. The fall crops have all gone bad, that's what that smell is."

The woman cried out with concern. Another woman spoke to the stout man urgently, "That's not what I was told. There was an accident in the medical facility, and now some people have gone missing."

Jennie tuned out the chatter around her. The chances were high that these statements were grossly inaccurate and nothing more than rumors spawned by desperate people seeking answers. They approached the square where a large crowd was gathering. Jennie's hand found Ethan's, and she interlaced her fingers in his. She linked her other arm with Belle's and noticed Belle put her arm around Travis' shoulder. At least now they couldn't get separated, Jennie thought.

They pressed forward into the dense crowd and tried to blend in. The four of them stood silently beside each other and looked up at the bell tower above the school. It was strange facing the school building where this had all begun for Jennie. The bell finally stopped tolling, and the crowd fell silent. The silence was deafening. Jennie trembled with anticipation. Ethan gently squeezed her hand and Belle pressed closer to her.

A figure emerged from the bell tower and stood on the roof of the schoolhouse. Jennie's mouth fell open, and the crowd around her murmured with confused sensationalism. This was not at all who Jennie had expected to see calling the Commune together. The name of the bold figure standing on the roof escaped Jennie's lips in a whisper, "Marlene."

Jennie had never seen Marlene look as she did now. She was not wearing the long purple robes of a Commune Elder, but she was wearing the lightweight leather armor of a warrior. The early sun silhouetted Marlene's body, and a blade hung from her belt. Marlene spoke in a voice that commanded the attention of everyone gathered.

"People of the Commune. You have all been taken for fools." Cries of protest spread through the crowd. Marlene held up her arms beckoning for silence. "There is darkness gathering at the wall. The lemerons are coming to destroy us. This is no accident. This is the work of another darkness which has taken root within the Commune."

Marlene paused and scanned the crowd. No one said a word. "There is a group of people seeking to overthrow the framework of our society. In doing so they have created – *created* – dociles. Anyone who has stood against them has been taken and forcefully turned into a mindless creature. James Townsend, Eleanor Townsend, Madam Marie, and Belle Joiner. All of these people were taken. If they are lucky, they are dead."

Jennie realized that Marlene wouldn't know yet that Belle was safe – at least for the time being. Jennie looked the crowd. The majority of the Commune people were completely fixated on Marlene and what she was saying. There were other people in the crowd who were moving deliberately toward the schoolhouse. Something about the way these people moved seemed threatening. *Could these be members of the Order?* Jennie wondered as a chill ran down her spine.

One of the people walking to the building stopped. It was a man with a hooked nose and he wore an expression of malice. He shouted up to Marlene. "Victor explained to us that these people wandered outside the walls and were taken by lemerons. There is no evidence that they were abducted by anyone here."

Another one of these people, presumably from the Order, stopped and shouted out, "That's right. Where is your proof?"

Belle cleared her throat as if she were about to speak. Jennie pulled her close and hissed "No," in her ear. Jennie knew that Belle could easily debunk what these Order people were claiming. Jennie must have missed the announcement that Belle supposedly wondered off and was taken by lemerons. "You do not want these people finding out that you escaped."

Belle nodded. "You're right. It's better that they think I'm still their prisoner," she whispered.

Jennie looked around the crowd again and saw that they were riled up. Confusion was giving way to frustration. Many in the crowd murmured agreement with the two people from the Order. Jennie's legs were quivering. Where were the Truth Seekers to offer the truth?

"Do not listen to them." Marlene barked. "*These* are the very people who have brought destruction to the Commune. They call themselves 'The Order' and they want nothing more than to destroy everything the Commune was built upon. Their plan is to slowly remove all those they deem undesirable. They feel that we, the undesirables, are syphoning their resources and pose a threat to them. They want to create a society full of mindless dociles where the Order members are the only ones who retain their free will."

The crowd was quiet again. Jennie's excitement was growing. Marlene was doing it. She was spreading the truth and actually doing something. Jennie eagerly looked at the faces around her and saw that her fellow townspeople were equally outraged by what they were hearing.

Marlene's voice rang out as clearly as the bell she had been ringing. "By abducting anyone who stands against the Order and by turning them into dociles, the Order has created a sensory beacon for the lemerons. The lemerons are drawn to the dociles as well as each other. I have been to the wall, and I have seen the storm that gathers there."

"What is the meaning of this?" A commanding male voice interrupted Marlene. Jennie looked in the direction of the voice, and there stood Victor on the steps of the Sanctuary. "My friends, do not fall for such folly. This tirade of Marlene's is preposterous and unfounded."

"Listen not to what this man says," Marlene shouted. "There are hundreds of lemerons gathering at the walls, and more are coming every day. This is all a direct result of the atrocities committed by the Order. Victor wants to call my claims baseless, because he is the leader of the Order. The smell in the air is the stench of the lemerons. If you do not believe me, let your nose decide. Go to the wall and see for yourselves if you must."

"Preposterous," Victor managed to say before the crowd drowned out his voice with angry shouts. Jennie saw her father, Jack Caraway, and a couple of farmers move toward Victor. They took hold of him, and Jack secured Victor's hands with rope. She felt a surge of pride that her father was on the right side. The crowd cheered as the corrupt Elder, Victor Glassman, was deposed.

Marlene raised her hand, and the crowd fell silent. "This started because of the creation of more dociles. This can end with the saving of the dociles. We are not beyond hope. We must no longer take ill advice from those who seek to destroy us from within. Only then can we continue our scientific research towards the reversal of the docile condition. Once we return them to their human state, the beacon within our walls which draws the lemerons to us will be no more."

Cheers of consent rose from the crowd. "Once we have achieved this, we can face the problem of the lemerons gathering at our wall. The wall is sound, but it may not keep out the growing number of lemerons for long," Marlene paused, as if to let the gravity of the situation sink in. "We require aide to defeat the lemerons. I must leave the Commune to seek out assistance from beyond the wall. I will return within a fortnight with our allies from the forest."

Indistinguishable questions filled the air from everyone talking at once. Jennie knew the people were likely reacting as Jennie had when she found Ethan and learned that they were not the last remaining humans. *She has done it.* Jennie thought with newfound respect for Marlene, *She held nothing back, everything is in the open now.* Jennie squeezed Ethan's hand to acknowledge that Marlene was talking about his people.

"She didn't abandon you," Jennie told Ethan. "Marlene thought it would be safer for you if you didn't remain here. She wanted to protect you from the Order."

Ethan looked at her with those green eyes that she adored, and he squeezed her hand. "Thank you. I'm starting to understand now," he said. "And I remember where I saw the horse symbol before." Ethan took the picture of him as a baby on Marlene's lap from his back pocket and let it fall open in his hand. "The symbol is a pendant she is wearing."

Jennie studied the photo with new eyes. Sure enough, hanging around Marlene's neck was the symbol of the rearing horse surrounded by a circle of leaves.

"I can't believe neither of us noticed it before," Jennie said. "Marlene knows what it means, I'm sure of it. It must be significant if she has it embossed on her journal and for her to wear around her neck."

"When I first met you, I said I probably wouldn't be able to stay here very long." Ethan's emerald eyes held deep remorse as he spoke. "Now that we have come this far and after everything that we've been through, I don't want to leave. I don't want to leave you." He looked up at the roof where Marlene was standing. "But there are too many questions that need to be answered."

"I understand," Jennie said. "If I had a second chance with my mother, I would take it too." Jennie watched as Marlene turned to enter the bell tower. "She will be looking for you in the forest, you know?"

"I know." Ethan nodded. "Not just me, but the rest of my people, too."

"And she could probably use our help out there against the lemerons."

"Our help?" Ethan raised an eyebrow and gave Jennie a playful smile.

Jennie returned the smile. "You didn't think you were going alone, did you?"

* * *

This is the end of Book One in
The Secret Archives Trilogy.
Keep an eye out for Book Two in 2019.

ACKNOWLEDGEMENTS

There are many people who supported me throughout the process of writing and publishing this book. Without them, this story might have never made it onto paper. I would like to thank my wonderful husband who encourages me to keep writing and to keep finding new stories to tell. My family has been behind me every step of the way for which I am eternally grateful.

I would like to thank the great people who helped transform the early workings of this story into a published book. Thank you to my beta readers who took time out of their busy lives to read this story and provide their valuable feedback. Thank you to Brass Rag Press and Juli's Elite Editing for providing their editing services. Thank you to the amazing Rene with Phycel Designs for making the interior of my book shine. Thank you to Covers by Christian for creating an amazing cover to help bring my vision to life.

A special thank you to my readers who chose to read this book. You have many books to choose from, and I am honored you selected my story. I sincerely hope you enjoyed reading this book. Thank you!

ABOUT THE AUTHOR

Valerie Puri has always had a lifelong interest in all forms of artistic expression. She has tried her hand at many things, yet she always finds her way back to reading and writing. With inspiration everywhere, Valerie finally put pen to paper (or rather, fingers to keyboard) with the intent of publishing her stories.

Writing has always come naturally to Valerie, and for a time she even worked as a technical writer. This experience and her current day job of project manager helps Valerie continue to hone her writing skills. Her true passion lies in the freedom that comes with writing the stories that pour from her imagination and real life inspiration.

Valerie believes that the experiences we have in life are just stories waiting to be written.

FOLLOW VALERIE

Website
www.valeriepuri.com

Facebook
www.facebook.com/authorvaleriepuri

Goodreads
www.goodreads.com/valeriepuri

Previous Works
The Crimson Tree
Second Chance in St. Louis